D0075554

EARTHDIVERS

The author expresses his gratitude
to the Graduate School
of the University of Minnesota
for research funds to complete this book.

EARTHDIVERS

Tribal Narratives on Mixed Descent

Gerald Vizenor

with illustrations by

Jaune Quick-to-See Smith

University of Minnesota Press • Minneapolis

Published by the University of Minnesota Press,
2037 University Avenue Southeast, Minneapolis, MN 55414
Printed in the United States of America

ISBN 0-8166-1048-7

In memory of

John Clement Beaulieu

and

Clement Vizenor

Contents

No matter how well educated an Indian may become, he or she always suspects that Western culture is not an adequate representation of reality. Life therefore becomes a schizophrenic balancing act wherein one holds that the creation, migration, and ceremonial stories of the tribe are true and that the Western European view of the world is also true . . . the trick is somehow to relate what one feels to what one is taught to think.

Vine Deloria, *The Metaphysics of Modern Existence*

The emphasis on individualism and liberal institutions, moreover, placed Indian tribalism in direct opposition to Americanism even more under democracy than under republicanism. Indians must join American society as individuals in the liberal state and economy rather than as tribes. Cultural assimilation, likewise, must proceed according to the values of individualism and not those of tribalism. What the proper White individual should be and therefore what the proper Indian individual must be represented an absolute antithesis to how Americans assumed Indians lived as tribal members. By definition, the tribal Indian lacked the industry, the self-reliance, and the material desires and success appropriate to the good American. Throughout the nineteenth century, missionaries and philanthropists, government officials in Washington and on the frontier, military officers and Western settlers measured the tribal Indian by their standard of Americanism and found him wanting . . . .

Robert Berkhofer, *The White Man's Indian*

Preface

> The fictional half-blood, like the fictional Indian, embodied both fact and myth, but in contrast to the Indian, he was not so readily depicted as either a "noble savage" or the barbaric antithesis to civilization. By his very nature the half-blood epitomized the integration . . . of the red and white races, provided a dramatic symbol of the benign possibilities or malign probabilities inherent in this encounter.
>
> William Scheick, *The Half-Blood*

Earthdivers, the title of this book of tribal narratives on mixed descent, is borrowed from a traditional theme in tribal creation myths and dedicated here as an imaginative metaphor.

The earthdivers in these twenty-one narratives are mixedbloods, or Métis, tribal tricksters and recast cultural heroes, the mournful and whimsical heirs and survivors from that premier union between the daughters of the woodland shamans and white fur traders. The Métis, or mixedblood, earthdivers in these stories dive into unknown urban places now, into the racial darkness in the cities, to create a new consciousness of coexistence.

Métis is a French word which means *mixedblood* in current usage, or a person of mixed Indian and French-Canadian ancestry. The Spanish word *mestizo* means a person of mixed Indian and European ancestry. The words *Métis* and *mixedblood* possess no social or scientific validation because blood mixture is not a measurement of consciousness, culture, or human experiences; but the word *Métis* is a source of notable and radical identification. Louis Riel, for example, one of the great leaders of the Métis, declared a new mixedblood nation in the last century. He was convicted of "high treason" and executed.

"It is true that our savage origin is humble, but it is meet that we honor our mothers as well as our fathers," said Louis Riel to his proud followers. He is quoted from *The Strange Empire of Louis Riel* by Joseph Kinsey Howard. "Why should we concern ourselves about what degree of mixture we possess of European or Indian blood? If we have ever so little of either gratitude or filial love, should we not be proud to say, *We are Métis.*"

Métis John Baptiste Cadotte was distinguished in tribal and white histories. William Whipple Warren noted in his *History of the Ojibway Nation* that Cadotte had "received a college education in Montreal. He was among the first individuals whose European, or white blood, became intermixed with the blood of the Ojibways. On leaving college, he became possessed of forty thousand francs which had been bequeathed to him by his father, and with this sum as capital, he immediately launched into the northwestern fur trade." Warren was educated in mission schools and was the first mixedblood to serve as a representative in the territorial legislature.

"Intermarriage went hand-in-glove with the trade in skins and furs from the first decades of discovery," writes Jacqueline Peterson in her brilliant essay "Prelude to Red River: A Social Portrait of the Great Lake Métis." She explains that the "core denominator of Métis identity was not participation in the fur trading network per se," but the mixedblood middleman "stance between Indian and European societies." The Métis "functioned not only as human carriers linking Indians and Europeans, but as buffers behind which the ethnic boundaries of antagonistic cultures remained relatively secure."

Jacqueline Peterson points out that "it is no coincidence that many of the labels describing the offspring of interracial unions articulate an implicit wish to blot out or sterilize the human consequences of miscegenation. Thus, like the derogation 'mulatto,' which stems from mule, and 'griffe,' the monstrous winged child of black and Indian parents, 'half-breed,' 'breed,' and 'mixed-blood' hint broadly at cultural and biological impotence."

In the traditional earthdiver creation myths the cultural hero or tribal trickster asked animals and birds to dive for the earth, but here, in the metaphor of the Métis earthdiver, white settlers are summoned to dive with mixedblood survivors into the unknown, into the legal morass of treaties and bureaucratic evils, and to swim deep down and around through federal exclaves and colonial economic enterprises in search of a few honest words upon which to build a new urban turtle island. In traditional stories and in these narratives the metaphor of the earthdiver centers on the *return* to the earth, rather than a *separation* from the earth and a futurist transcendence to a computerized heaven. The earthdiver does not dive into space. The trickster secures his earth, his urban places now, and then he dreams out of familiar time and space. Métis tricksters and earthdrivers are the metaphors between new sources of opposition and colonial ideas about savagism and civilization.

The earthdiver myth has a "word-wide distribution," according to the folklorist Elli Kaija Köngäs in an article published in *Ethnohistory*. "It is told in various forms, but it always has four invariable traits—earth covered with water, the creator, the diver, and the making of the earth. . . ."

In his book *The Religions of the American Indians*, Åke Hultkrantz writes that the "primal sea represents primordial chaos, while the great flood is chaos of a later date, caused, for example, by the wrath of a god or the transgression of a taboo . . . . No other creation myth in North America is as extensive as the one about the Earth Diver who brings up land from the primal water . . . .

"In North America there is a profusion of tales regarding the origin of the world, whereas the creation of man is a rarer topic. . . . One of these traditions, which is prevalent in North America and well known in North Asia and Europe, tells how the creator sent an animal down to the bottom of the sea to bring up sand or mud from which the earth was subsequently made. . . ."

Earl Count in his essay "The Earth-Diver and the Rival Twins: A Clue to Time Correlation in North-Eurasiatic and North American Mythology," published in *The Civilizations of Ancient America*, states that the "cosmogonic notion of a primal sea out of which a diver fetches material for making dry land, is easily among the most widespread single concepts held by man."

In his provocative research article "Earth-Diver: Creation of the Mythopoeic Male," published in *American Anthropologist*, Alan

Dundes turns his attention from modern myths to psychoanalytic theories and assumes, for the purposes of his hypothesis, the "existence of a cloacal theory of birth; and the existence of pregnancy envy on the part of males." While Dundes waits to be invited to *dive,* in the metaphorical sense of the urban earthdiver, through his own assumptions and ideas, consider one version of an earthdiver myth as an illustration of the creation of turtle island. Creation myths are not time bound, the creation takes place in the telling, in present-tense metaphors.

Victor Barnouw collected earthdiver creation stories at Lac du Flambeau and published them in his book *Wisconsin Chippewa Myths and Tales.* Barnouw writes that the narrator of the following earthdiver myth was a shaman, or tribal spiritual leader, "to whom I have given the pseudonym of Tom Badger . . . a quiet level-headed man in his seventies, with a good sense of humor."

Wenebojo is also transcribed as *manibozho, nanibozhu, wanibozhu, manabozho, nanabozho, nanabush,* and other variations from the oral tradition. *Naanabozho* is the compassionate tribal trickster of the woodland *anishinaabeg,* the people named the Chippewa, Ojibway, Ojibwa, or Ojibwe. *Wenebojo* or *naanabozho* is the *compassionate* trickster, not the trickster in the word constructions of the anthropologist Paul Radin, the one who "possesses no values, moral or social . . . knows neither good nor evil yet is responsible for both," but the imaginative trickster, the one who cares to balance the world between terminal creeds and humor with unusual manners and ecstatic strategies.

Wenebojo was standing on the top of the tree . . . and the water was up to his mouth. Pretty soon Wenebojo felt that he wanted to defecate. He couldn't hold it. The shit floated up to the top of the water and floated around his mouth. . . .

Wenebojo noticed that there was an animal in the water. . . . Then he saw several animals—beaver, muskrat, and otter. Wenebojo spoke to the otter first.

"Brother," he said, "could you go down and get some earth? If you do that, I will make an earth for you and me to live on. . . ."

Away he went to the bottom of the water. . . . He drowned. Then he floated to the top. Wenebojo tried to reach the otter. He got hold of him finally and looked into the otter's paws and mouth, but he didn't find any dirt. Then Wenebojo blew on the otter, and the otter came to again. Wenebojo asked him, "Did you see anything?"

"No," said the otter.

The next person Wenebojo spoke to was the beaver. He asked him to go after some earth down below and said, "If you do, I'll make an earth for us to live on. . . ."

The beaver was gone a long time. Pretty soon he floated to the top of the water. He also drowned. Wenebojo got hold of the beaver and blew on him. When he came to, Wenebojo examined his paws and mouth to see if there was any dirt there, but he couldn't find anything. He asked the beaver, "Did you see any earth at the bottom?"

"Yes, I did," said the beaver. "I saw it, but I couldn't get any of it."

These animals had tried and failed. . . .

The muskrat was playing around there too. Wenebojo didn't think much about the muskrat, since he was so small; but after a while he said to him, "Why don't you try and go after some of that dirt too?"

The muskrat said, "I'll try," and he dived down.

Wenebojo waited and waited a long time for the muskrat to come up to the top of the water. When he floated up to the top, he was all crippled. Wenebojo caught the muskrat and looked him over. The muskrat had his paws closed up tight. His mouth was shut too. Wenebojo opened the muskrat's front paw and found a grain of earth in it. He took it. In his other front paw he found another little grain, and one grain of dirt in each of his hind paws. There was another grain in his mouth.

When he found these five grains, Wenebojo started to blow on the muskrat, blew on him until he came back to life. Then Wenebojo took the grains of sand in the palm of his hand and held them up to the sun to dry them out. When the sand was all dry, he threw it around onto the water. There was a little island then.

They went onto the little island—Wenebojo, the beaver, the otter, and the muskrat. Wenebojo got more earth on the island and threw it all around. The island got bigger. It got larger every time

Wenebojo threw out another handful of dirt. Then animals at the bottom of the water, whoever was there, all came up to the top of the water and went to the island where Wenebojo was. They were tired of being in the water all that time, and when they heard about the earth that Wenebojo had made, they all wanted to stay there.
Wenebojo kept on throwing earth around.

Dundes observes that despite the "lack of a great number of actual excremental myths, the existence of any at all would appear to lend support to the hypothesis that men do think of creativity in anal terms, and further that this conception is projected into mythical cosmogonic terms."

Dundes continues his comments on excremental expansion: "The fecal nature of the particle is also suggested by its magical expansion. One could imagine that as one defecates one is thereby creating an ever-increasing amount of earth."

We are fortunate, perhaps, as Métis and mixedblood earthdivers, that Alan Dundes did not choose to explain creation in terms of female penile envies, or penis captivus, and the expansion of urine as a theoretical assumption to account for the flood. Expanding his discussion to include ideas from the tradition of philosophical dualism, Dundes asserts that the "devil is clearly identified with matter and in particular with defecation. In a phrase, it is the devil who does the dirty work."

Victor Barnouw does not seem to resist these mythic movements or rise above fecal interpretations of tribal creation stories. In a section of his book devoted to *anal themes* he writes that "Alan Dundes has suggested that the Earth-Diver motif is a male fantasy of creation stemming from male envy of female pregnancy and an assumed cloacal theory of birth. In Dundes' view the mud from which the earth is formed is symbolic of feces. This may seem an extravagant hypothesis, but it would be in keeping with Chippewa myth that its exclusion of women and its striking anal themes. . . . The idea of creating people from feces occurs in some Chippewa tales . . . in our series Wenebojo creates some Indian warriors by defecation here and there and sticking feathers into turds."

Barnouw refers to other stories in his discussion of *anal themes,* including one where the daughter of a chief denies her suitors. The suitors, "in revenge, defecate into a hole, make a human form from the dung, dress it up in fine clothes, and will that it become a human being. The dung man goes to the village, where the chief's daughter falls in love with him. He leaves, and the girl follows his tracks. She finally comes to a pile of dung, where the trail ends. . . . In both of these stories males create people by defecating, in line with Dundes' hypothesis."

Some anthropologists seem to have little appreciation for sacred games in tribal creations. Their secular seriousness separates the tribes from humor, from untimed metaphors, and the academic intensities of career bound anthropologists approach diarrhetic levels of terminal theoretical creeds. The creation myth that anthropologists never seem to tell is the one where *naanabozho,* the cultural trickster, made the first anthropologist from fecal matter. Once made, more were cloned in graduate schools from the first fecal creation of an anthropologist.

Martin Bear Charme, founder of the Landfill Meditation Reservation and the seminar with the same name, scooped the oil from his outsized nose with his dark middle finger, his habit once or twice an hour, and spread the viscid mounds over his cuticles. Sitting near the window, one would never know, watching his smooth hands in backward speech, that the refuse meditator was reservation born, once poor and undereducated for urban survival.

Métis Bear Charme is an earthdiver. He studied welding on a federal relocation program, but scrap connections bored him so the urban earthdiver turned to scavenging and made a fortune hauling and filling wetlands with solid waste and urban swill. Once a worthless mud flat, his lush refuse reservation is now worth millions.

Métis Charme the earthdiver made his own turtle island. His legal adviser has petitioned the federal government for recognition of the island as a sovereign tax-free meditation nation, a place where laws and liens are intuitive.

While the traditional earthdiver themes have been exhausted in minor academic word wars, the mixedblood earthdiver is a metaphor in a timeless tribal drama. Turtle island is an imaginative place; not a formula, but a metaphor which connects dreams to the earth. The Métis are divided in white consciousness, denied an absolute cultural corner, and, therefore, spared from extinction in word and phrase museums.

Métis earthdivers and new urban shamans now summon the white world to dive, to dive deep and return with the sacred earth. The Métis wait above the chaos at common intersections in the cities for the white animals to return with the earth, enough to build a new urban turtle island. Earthdivers, tricksters, shamans, poets, dream back the earth.

"We demand too much when we ask that the poet establish a new world," writes Karsten Harries in his article "Metaphor and Transcendence." The world seems to float on words, but "first we have to learn to listen more attentively to the many voices of the earth. What makes such listening difficult is the fact that as members of a community we are necessarily caught up in already-established and taken-for-granted ways of speaking and seeing.

"We understand things without having made them our own. The adequacy of words is taken for granted, their origin forgotten. There are moments when the inadequacy of our language seizes us, when language seems to fall apart and falling apart opens us to what transcends it. . . . As language falls apart, contact with being is reestablished. . . ."

Métis earthdivers speak a new language, their experiences and dreams are metaphors, and in some urban places the earthdivers speak backwards to be better heard and understood on the earth. Father Bearald One, Doctor Peter Fountain, Martin Bear Charme, Happie Comes Last, Rubie Blue Welcome, Mouse Proof Martin, and other characters in these narratives speak unusual languages, so unusual that "language seems to fall apart," but this illusion of disintegration, Karsten Harries asserts, "does not lead to silence. . . ."

In his essay on "What Metaphors Mean" Donald Davidson writes that "metaphor is the dreamwork of language and, like all dreamwork, its interpretation reflects as much on the interpreter as on the originator. The interpretation of dreams requires collaboration between a dreamer and a waker, even if they be the same person; and the act of interpretation is itself a work of the imagination.

"So too understanding a metaphor is as much a creative endeavor as making a metaphor, and as little guided by rules. . . . The idea, then, is that in metaphor certain words take on new, or what are often called 'extended,' meanings. . . . Perhaps, then, we can explain metaphor as a kind of ambiguity: in the context of a metaphor, certain words have either a new or an original meaning, and the force of the metaphor depends on our uncertainty as we waver between the two meanings. . . ."

Métis earthdivers waver and forbear extinction in two worlds. Métis are the force in the earthdiver metaphor, the tension in the blood and the uncertain word, the imaginative and compassionate trickster on street corners in the cities. When the mixedblood earthdiver summons the white world to dive like the otter and beaver and muskrat in search of the earth, and federal funds, he is both animal and trickster, both white and tribal, the uncertain creator in an urban metaphor based on a creation myth that preceded him in two world views and oral traditions.

Métis, *naanabozho* tells, were the first earthdivers.

Tribal ideas and sources of consciousness, and earthdiver metaphors, demand some privities on tribal world views: time is circular and creation takes place in ceremonies and between tellers and listeners; sacred names, dreams, and visions are images that connect the bearer to the earth; shamans and other tribal healers and visionaries speak the various languages of plants and animals and feel the special dream power to travel backward from familiar times and places.

A. Irving Hallowell has written numerous descriptive and research articles about woodland *anishinaabeg*. His stories are familiar to most listeners. For example, he once asked an old *anishinaabe* man about the animation of stones:

"Are *all* the stones we see about us alive? He reflected for a long while and then replied, 'No! But *some* are.' This qualified answer made a lasting impression on me. And it is thoroughly consistent with other data that indicate that the Ojibwa are not animists in the sense that they dogmatically attribute living souls to inanimate objects such as stones."

In his article "Ojibwa Ontology, Behavior, and World View," Hallowell explains that his tribal friends were "puzzled by the white man's conception of thunder and lightning as natural phenomena as they were by the idea that the earth is round and flat.

I was pressed on more than one occasion to explain thunder and lightning, but I doubt whether my somewhat feeble efforts made much sense to them. . . . My explanations left their own beliefs completely unshaken. . . . Underlying the Ojibwa view there may be a level of naive perceptual experience that should be taken into account. . . . What is particularly interesting is that the avian nature of the Thunder Bird does not rest solely on an arbitrary image. Phenomenally, thunder does exhibit 'behavioral' characteristics that are analogous to avian phenomena in this region."

Hallowell did not have to talk to old men to learn that the earth and other forms of life are personal experiences. Some anthropologists separate themselves from the earth and imagination with colonial research words and elitist templates. The earthdivers now turn around, talk backward, and summon the anthropologists to dive for the earth with imaginative words.

"The Ojibwa self is not oriented to a behavioral environment in which a distinction between human beings and supernatural beings is stressed. . . . *Impersonal* forces are never the causes of events. *Somebody* is always responsible," Hallowell points out in his book *Culture and Experience.*

The names of the characters in these twenty-one narratives are real and imagined, but it will be difficult to know the differences. Real characters seem fictional, at times, more imagined; the text identities of several fictional characters seem real in imagined places. The real worlds are not unlike imagined mythic worlds. Differences in realities are never clear because the distances between tribal dreams, earthdiver myths, comedies and metaphors, and familiar places float free from time in some conversations.

"For those of us whose vision is ineluctably drawn toward contemplating the mystery dimension of life," writes Stephen Larsen in his book *The Shaman's Doorway,* "myth does not require explanation, but attention. Myth is the ever-changing mask that the mind of the beholder fits over a reality he has never truly seen."

Clement Beaulieu is the created name for the author, who appears, as he did in his last book *Wordarrows: Indians and Whites in the New Fur Trade,* in several narratives. The use of a created name for the author avoids the limitations suggested in autobiographical writing and the use of first-person pronouns. However, other critical textual considerations are raised when an author writes about himself through any name as a character in a narrative. Georges Gusdorf expresses with unusual ease the consciousness of the autobiographer in his article "Conditions and Limits of Autobiography," which was translated by James Olney and published in his book *Autobiography: Essays Theoretical and Critical.*

"The man who takes delight in thus drawing his own images believes himself worthy of a special interest. Each of us tends to think of himself as the center of a living space: I count, my existence is significant to the world, and my death will leave the world incomplete. . . .

"This consciousness awareness of the singularity of each individual life is the late product of a specific civilization. Through most of human history, the individual does not oppose himself to all others; he does not feel himself to exist outside of others, and still less against others, but very much *with* others in an interdependent existence that asserts its rhythms everywhere in the community."

Métis earthdivers are the new metaphors between communal tribal cultures and the cultures that oppose traditional connections, the cultures that would own and market the earth. The experiences of the autobiographer are similar to those of the earthdiver: the blood wavers in personal metaphors.

"It is obvious that autobiography is not possible in a cultural landscape where consciousness of self does not . . . exist," writes Gusdorf. "But this unconsciousness of personality, characteristic of primitive societies such as enthnologists describe to us, lasts also in more advanced civilizations that subscribe to mythic structures, they too being governed by the principles of repetition. . . .

"Autobiography becomes possible only under certain metaphysical preconditions. To begin with, at the cost of a cultural revolution, humanity must have emerged from the mythic framework of traditional teachers and must have entered into the perilous domain of history. The man who takes the trouble to tell of himself knows that the present differs from the past and that it will not be repeated in the future; he has become more aware of differences than similarities. . . .

"Artistic creation is a struggle with an angel, in which the creator is the more certain of being vanquished since the opponent is still himself. He wrestles with his shadow, certain only of never laying hold of it. . . ."

Clement Beaulieu wrestles like an earthdiver with his shadow; he captures some light from the written images of his experiences. The opposition of the trickster, and the implied resolutions, are internal; anarchism is balanced in dreams and mythic imagination. The verbal contradance is more than a mere autobiographical cakewalk.

"There is no question but that a spirit of anarchism is bred within the autobiographical act," writes Louis Renza in his article "A Theory of Autobiography." The sense of anarchism is "mitigated in words where the writer blends the exclusive sense of self disclosed through his act into an exclusive, though collective, 'minority' persona."

Clement is the first name of my father, who was born mixedblood on the White Earth Reservation, and died downtown like an earthdiver; and the first name of several distant relatives. Beaulieu, from Alice Beaulieu Vizenor, is the last name, the birth name, of my paternal grandmother who was also born on the White Earth Reservation.

Frank Premack is the name of a real person, an unusual man of intense humor and compassion, who, at the time of his death, was an investigative reporter for the *Minneapolis Tribune.* When he was the City Editor of the newspaper, Premack demanded that we find stories to keep alive a capital punishment issue until the death sentence for Thomas James White Hawk was commuted to life imprisonment. Premack demanded this coverage, notwithstanding criticism from other editors. Premack possessed a brilliant skepticism about politicians, intuitive energies that earned him the praise of his profession. He was also a sensitive and comical clown who once climbed on top of his desk to demonstrate to all writers how to "shorten a story written by Gerald Vizenor." He cut a five-page feature news story in half and printed the bottom part. Premack said too often that the "second coming is worth no more than a page and a half."

The first story on the funeral of Dane Michael White was published November 21, 1968, on the front page of the *Minneapolis Tribune.* Comments attributed to Senator Walter Mondale appeared November 26, 1968, and other stories about the suicide death of Dane Michael White followed for several weeks.

"The Chair of Tears," the first narrative in this book, deserves some comment. The place and the issues revealed are real; higher education has been unsupportive of tribal studies, but not unsympathetic, a case of liberal manners without commitment; but the characters, familiar as some would seem, are fictional names and do *not* represent real persons at colleges and universities where the author has taught.

The author prefers the word *tribal* over other names for tribal people and cultures unless those names, such as *anishinaabe,* are transcribed from tribal languages. The word *Indian,* of course, is an invention which has rendered extinct thousands of individual and distinct tribal cultures. While it is cumbersome to use the word *indian* in lower case letters in all twenty-one narratives, the author uses *indian* in the last narratives in the book to illustrate racial and cultural invalidations.

There are limitations to the use of the word *tribal,* because the word suggests a colonial and political derogation of oral traditional and communal cultures. Notwithstanding the colonial usage, the author intends the word *tribal* to be a celebration of communal values which connect the *tribal celebrants* to the earth.

Words from the language of the *anishinaabe,* or the plural *anishinaabeg,* are italicized for emphasis. The phonetic transcription of the words, outside of quotations, follows the entries in *Ojibwewi-ikidowinan: An Ojibwe Word Resource Book,* edited by John Nichols and Earl Nyholm, and published at Bemidji State University.

The cover art and the illustrations were created for this book by Jaune Quick-To-See Smith. She was born in Montana of French-Cree and Shoshone descent, studied at Olympic College in Washington, Framingham State College in Massachusetts, the University of New Mexico, and now lives in Albuquerque. Her artistic imagination is a special voice which soars through mythic time and sacred tribal memories.

"My feelings about my ethnicity and the land build metaphors . . . a language of my own for events which take place on the prairie," said Quick-To-See about her work. "I place my markings onto a framework in homage to the ancient travois: in a sense, piling my dreams on for a journey across the land. Smears and stains of pigments with the crudeness of charcoal feel aboriginal and prehistoric to me."

The author is indebted to his friends, listeners, tricksters, and humorists, and fine tellers of stories in the oral tradition. Special appreciation is expressed to my son, Robert Vizenor, for his trust and praise; and to Terry Wilson, who has a rich and generous sense of humor; to Ronald Libertus and Greg Young for their support; to Clarke Chambers for his thoughtful encouragement; and to Dallas Chrislock and Ruth Bauer at the Minnesota Historical Society. Special thanks to Gerri Balter who demonstrated her fine sense of humor while she typed the final manuscript, and thanks to Bonnie Wallace, Timothy Dunnigan, David Beaulieu, and Sheila Levine.

"The comic mode of human behavior represented in literature is the closest art has come to describing man as an adaptive animal," writes Joseph Meeker in his book *The Comedy of Survival: Studies in Literary Ecology*. "The humor of comedy is most often an attempt to deflate the overinflated, not to trivialize what is genuinely important. . . . In literature or in ecology, comedy enlightens and enriches human experience without trying to transform either mankind or the world."

Wenebojo kept on throwing earth around.

Gerald Vizenor
Minneapolis, Minnesota

X+Y = X+Y/2
294/5000
?
CUT HERE
DELETE
2864
-183

EARTHDIVERS IN HIGHER EDUCATION

The Chair of Tears

It is a mistake to think that human beings always seek stability and order. Anyone who is open to experience must recognize that order is transient. . . . Because change occurs and is inevitable, we become anxious. Anxiety drives us to seek security, or, on the contrary, adventure. . . . The study of fear is therefore not limited to the study of withdrawal and retrenchment . . . it also seeks to understand growth, daring, and adventure.

Yi-Fu Tuan, *Landscapes of Fear*

General George Armstrong Custer was hospitalized for observation in a mental ward three weeks after he was killed at the battle of the Little Bighorn when a mule skinner found him alone in the hills under a whole moon browsing with several ruminant mammals.

"General, sir, what are you doing here?"

"Seeking my ultimate vision."

"But, sir, not with these sheep."

"Soldier, there are simple sheep and there are superior sheep, but you are talking to a presidential supersheep," said the general as he unbuttoned his bloodstained uniform and exposed his bare rump and chest.

"But, sir . . ." stammered the soldier as he slapped his hands to his cheeks, "what is that tattoo on your chest, sir, and on your bottom?"

General Custer, resurrected on four cloven hoofs, turned to the moon and revealed the tattooed faces of several tribal warriors on his chest and sheared rump and shoulders.

The soldier saluted the warriors.

Classified advertisements, said the conference scholar turning his attention from satirical stories to salutations and explanations, hold more adventure and imagination than the word castles built from stale conversations between scholars, but an invitation to deliver a paper at a warm place in the middle of winter is reason enough to abandon academic fear and idealism.

Clement Beaulieu, mixedblood tribal writer and college teacher, told those attending the conference on *Mythic Satire and Secular Reversals* that his presentation would not include structural or critical commentaries. Instead, he scrapped the academic models, thrust his head from behind the podium like a crow in a lookout tree, and read an imaginative satirical narrative about mythic resurrection and tribal studies departments.

Captain Shammer, ladies and gentlemen, is the satirical character who has traveled with me, and with several warriors and generals, in these stories. Shammer, as the name seems to suggest, *sham, shame, shammer, shaman,* is a person of *magical ethos,* a theme developed by Robert Elliot in his book *The Power of Satire*. Shammer is the mixedblood spur on the moral tribal weapons, visions from unusual times and places, in these stories, or, to borrow a few phrases from Elliot, an underground constitutive "connection of satire with magical power. . . ."

The magical satire starts with a resurrected general on the browse out of time and place, and a tribal trickster dressed in the uniform of a general, ritual clowns bearing the estranged mask of General George Custer. The general called cadence on a walk bridge over the dead river and browsed on campus.

Shammer is the trickster with martial masks, and his appearance on campus as a resurrected general did not seem to surprise simple or superior students and scholars. He was, in fact, saluted several times on the mall, and he was asked on the elevator in the social sciences tower how the weather was in the tribal world. Thunderstorms, he said, and the prairie browse is higher than it has ever been in tribal histories.

Shammer marched in masks to celebrate ironies and the academic contradictions of his appointment as chairman of the Department of American Indian Studies. The troubled search committee members, exhausted from their political duties, reversed the obvious procedure and settled on the person with the *least* credentials, the lowest on the list of applicants, because the previous six chairs were all experts, specialists in their narrow word corners, and failures. Academic standards crack like frozen underwear when tribal tricksters cut a shorter path beneath the bottom line. What is sham and falseness should fail, not what is specialized truth, but the trickster, at times, becomes a reluctant hero in these stories because he neither asked nor applied to teach or to chair. His name was dropped, without his knowledge, on a piece of plain brown paper. Shammer became a sacred and secular academic reversal in tribal time.

Captain Shammer served as chair for less than three weeks, but in that time he accomplished more through inversion and diversion than had all his predecessors. The episodes during his tenure in the department are tribal contraries in a satirical contradance.

Captain Shammer took hold of the well-worn pink plastic mixedblood reins and rode the old red wagon constellations proud as a tribal trickster through the ancient word wars, with mule skinners and ruminant mammals, behind academic lines. In seven sorties, he altered the department, drew tears and humor, becalmed audiences, and disappeared before he was challenged or paid for his time.

There are no saints in the academic tribal world, nothing is perfect, but Captain Shammer came as close as one dares to be a heroic tribal figure. He founded the *Halfbreed Hall of Fame*, but it was not until his portrait appeared in a special exhibition on warriors by artist Jan Attridge that the seventh chairman of the department was named to his own *Halfbreed Hall of Fame*.

The actual administrative decree from the search committee and the academic dean was telephoned during a thunderstorm, and parts of the surprise message, including the unusual conditions of his appointment as chairman of the department, were lost to lightning, static, and electronic whistles.

The next morning, two hours into his appointment, Shammer announced at his first of seven press conferences that he had offered for sale to the highest bidder the whole Department of American Indian Studies.

"Next week, in the morning, at the seventh and last news conference," Chairman Shammer announced several times to the two incredulous reporters in his bookless eighth-floor storage room overlooking the river, "we will open the sealed bids and reveal the new owner of the department, lock, stock, and on the barrel head."

"But how?"

"Cash, of course, hot cash, per capita payments to the survivors, those who have taught and studied, more and less, in the department, even the students who have completed their incompletes," Shammer explained. He sat on his bare black desk with his small mixedblood hands driven deep into his pants pockets.

The announcement, later identified in a committee investigative report on *Mental Separations in Higher Tribal Education*, as his "first of seven deranged decisions as chairman," circulated word over whispered word in white conversations from door to door and floor to floor, over the river and under the bridge in fast talk until the embellished news stopped, like fat flies on tanglefoot paper, in the right ear of the academic dean, while we were on the elevator rising to lunch at the Faculty Club.

"Then the savage sold the office equipment," an informant told on the elevator, "sailed the files from the eighth floor, set the clock to tribal time, closing time, pulled the plug, and then he issued blankets, doubled all salaries, and turned the department into a brothel."

"Wish fulfillment?" asked a colleague.

"Perhaps this can be a model for termination."

"Terrific, sell the reservations, too," said a sociologist.

"Red flag the bastards."

Captain Shammer was the first chair to recognize that fast stories about tribal troubles in higher education are the structural substitutes for adventures on the mythical frontier. Book-bound white scholars fast draw the woodland savages with words on the elevator, better on the up elevator. Troubles in the department continue in a sacred game for the pleasures of new academic frontiers.

"Remarkable," said Dean Colin Defender in a voice as crisp as a fresh white radish. "All *that* happened before lunch on the first day in the chair. . . . We need that man in central administration, give me his name."

"The new chairman where no chair holds."

"Chairs never hold thin."

"Chairman of what?"

"Anthropology," said a passenger.

"No, no, economics, he must be from economics."

"Tribal shit," said a cynic from the physical plant as the elevator shuddered and stopped on the top floor. The door opened and conversations on the elevator meshed in perfect academic time with similar stories in the lunch line. An example of structural imagination and unusual mindless harmonies.

"Well, my good fellow," said a stout professor of education as he stepped from the elevator, "your description did not exclude current economic theories."

"That new chairman was seen on the bridge last night by several students from my class," said a professor three bodies back in the lunch line. "He wore a disguise, a long blonde wig, and was dressed in the uniform of a general with his sword drawn, it was reported, and he asked for directions to the White House."

"Was it *not* Vine Deloria, the tribal diatribist," hummed a man from the medical school, "who published a book entitled *Custer Died for Your Sins*?" No one in the lunch line caught the connection or the meaning of his reference, not even his laughter, to the behavior of the new chairman. Notwithstanding the caverns between cultural images, the courteous scholars smiled and nodded in line like stout bullheads hooked on breadball bait.

"Not, it was *not* . . ."

"Not what?"

"Double negatives form a positive, but there are no speakers who form a negative from double positives," said a distinguished professor from the side of his mouth near the end of the line.

"Yeah, yeah," said a tall research assistant.

Dean Colin Defender, better known to his colleagues in the Department of Forest Resources as Slash and Burn, so named for his fiscal policies when he became dean, smiled in line on time. "Yeah, yeah, yeah," he said underbreath. Slash and Burn has an unusual smile, a professional private school class conscious smile, practiced to whip or spread best where there is little humor. The dean stands low, more like an ornamental shrub, bald and burned on the top of his ears, but with his head thrust back like a grackle and his chest and short branches advanced he appears much more substantial in a lunch line.

"What happened this morning, difficult as it is to believe, was a *real* decision on the campus," explained Slash and Burn while he shifted to his lecture posture, fingertips tucked beneath his belt, thumbs exposed over his stomach. "Chairman Shammer would like to sell the Department of American Indian Studies."

"Fat chance," snapped a librarian.

"Readable stories," asserted a punctual associate dean, "but who, pray tell, who would take that place even with subsidies? Not only that, but selling the department is like selling a mortgaged mental ward."

Slash and Burn smiled and then continued his lecture as he shuffled forward in the lunch line. "Shammer was hired with no interview, no application, no known academic credentials, because the department wanted an unknown mixedblood . . . to know people in the tribal world is to mistrust them.

"Shammer is the seventh chair in the past three years, who can tell what will happen with an unknown, we have nothing to lose. . . . He was appointed because no one found fault with him during the selection process.

"Now, first morning on campus, he intends to sell the place to the highest bidder," explained Slash and Burn, true to his name, "which could prove to be a unique means of involving the private sector and reduce our fiscal obligations to the department. On the other hand, what he has announced is not much different from other departments soliciting federal and corporate funds for research. Higher education has always been for sale on both ends, research and instruction; the difference here is that this new chair, part cracker, might I add, is seeking the highest, *not* the lowest, bids.

"But the trouble with American Indian Studies is that the liberal market has vanished like a handful of tribal maize at a grain exchange; real grain and real trouble never did sell well." Slash and Burn smiled, pulled his fingers from beneath his belt, and then examined several forks before choosing the one with an appropriate bend to fit his narrow mouth. Conversations behind him in the lunch line turned to inflation and salaries.

The Department of American Indian Studies has died several times in the hands of students, committees, and faculties, in the past decade. First the students wanted traditional-minded teachers, then the instructors wanted institutional scholars to impress the administration, but the students forced the scholars out and demanded a chairman who had experiences in tribal communities, urban and reservation. The deans remained silent, hesitant colonialists, waiting for the tribal dust to clear from internal stress. Tribal troubles stimulated conversations in the lunch line and benefited the administration: the spoils from the internal tribal word wars became office space and salaries.

The chair is referred to as the *chair of tears*.

Last rites were celebrated over six chair graves, bundles of notes and memoranda were buried in white boxes, but contradictions in higher education, like shamans in the underworld, are dissolved with resurrected chairs.

Captain Shammer, the most recent to sit in the resurrected chair —all chairs but the first, the founder, were mixedbloods—was hired without an interview because to see was to disagree and the department could not survive more discordance. He knew even less about the department than the department knew about him. His unusual perceptions were based on personal philosophies and on his observations of farm animals and ant colonies. For example, he told several students on the bridge one night that his decisions were based on contraries, "in the white face of the most obvious, the opposite must be done . . . remember that when there is trouble in the ranks the ants first remove their dead warriors."

When the department was first organized it was impossible to avoid the white hands of paternalism, but now, seven chairs later, the administration has little to do with the department, avoiding most contacts, an enlightened liberal posture to leave the savages to their own internal troubles. Viewed as a marriage, the department would have a good divorce case, based on abandonment and mental cruelties.

Captain Shammer arrived on the first morning as chairman with a large red pack on his back and a languid blonde woman laced to his left arm.

"Direct me to the prime roost," he said as he unshouldered his pack and unfingered his blonde. "Where should we start unloading the red wagon of supercharms and market dreams?"

Little Ramon, the departmental secretary, lifted from his chair in slow motions, his mouth opened wide to speak, but his lips rolled and his pink tongue wagged without a sound. Ramon, mixedblood black, boasts more about his being homosexual than about his racial mixture. He was hired by the late chair number five, a tribal woman, who thought a black male homosexual would reduce political intrigues in the department. Malignant gossip, in contrast to humanistic chatter, had become a new tribal disease under academic pressure.

Ramon, meanwhile, should have vanished when the committee fired number five, but in a few months he managed to gather enough dirt and sweet soap dialogue on persons in high places to maintain his position. Now, at the center of tribal rumors and bad dreams, the talebearer tender was unable to speak.

"Put the sacred tree down, sweetheart," said the chairman number seven. "This man here must think we are a bit weird to be packing a dead tree around with us. Put it down and we can tell stories about the races and the trees until he understands."

"Not at all," the secretary snapped like a thin black crow cocked behind his desk. "Let me guess, you must be Doctor Captain Shammer, our new chairman, times seven."

"No. . . ."

"Splendid," exclaimed Little Ramon.

"No, on the doctor part, mister," explained the new chairman, "but yes, yes, on the rest. Now, please direct me to the withered roost."

"How strange does the world turn."

"Interesting enough," responded chairman seven. "Do you know what interested me today? Well, what interested me is how the tribal world could have been created on the back of a turtle. . . . Think about that, have you ever tried to pack mud on the back of a turtle?"

"Not in recent time."

"Take my word for it then, that turtleback talk is nothing more than another one of those stories." Shammer pulled his thumb and finger down the corner of his mouth in preparation for more stories. "Think about that, mister secretary. . . . Now take this dead tree here, let me tell you about that. . . ."

"Please, forgive me for not escorting you sooner to your office, or roost as you call it, which is right out here, down the hall. . . . Please, follow me now," said Ramon as he stepped out of the main office and walked down the hall to the storage room. "You might have thought that the large office next to mine was the roost, and indeed it once was, but since the last chair, number six, no one will enter or settle in that office."

"Superstitious?"

"Well, what we have done is to move our office machines and materials into the main roost, and then we turned the supplies room into the *real* roost for you; while you are here, this will be your place. . . . Your turtle roost, so to speak."

"Sweetheart, remember the sacred tree."

The founder of the department, the first chair, the wise man, the one who created the academic world for tribal studies, was tall, stout, and a fullblood traditional dancer. He wore ribbon shirts, leathers, bound his black hair in braids and was trusted and respected in the oral tradition as a tribal scholar in all places, at all times, on reservations and in the cities; but conservative administrators were cautious, unconvinced colonialists, and the tribal founder was denied tenure because he was not well published.

"He was a fine brush man," Slash and Burn explained, "but he was not and never will be a scholar." The dean, overbeaded with white expectations on tribal dreams, appointed a committee to investigate the department, a political decision to avoid direct support of tribal studies.

The Internal Review Committee reported that "where we feared that we would find an intellectually and academically strangled unit with a *garrison mentality*, we found instead a healthy and forward-looking department. The grade inflation in the Department of American Indian Studies seems especially severe over the last few years. In some part this may be due to the special academic needs of American Indian students.

"As the University decides on the nature of its commitment, it will have to come to terms with a historical fact that emerged to us repeatedly in our discussions: that the burst of *romantic* appreciation of things Indian seems to be waning, seemingly both within the Indian communities and elsewhere. While such a passing of the romantic phase might well be seen to have alarming enrollment implications for the Department of American Indian Studies, this committee was pleased that members of the department seemed generally comforted by the new trends."

So ends the first chair.

The second chairman of the department was the first tribal knight who rode a proud horse, he was well published to please the administration, appointed with tenure, and decorated in academic circles, but some radical urban students did not like the wine he drank and the clothes he wore. The first knight was isolated and cursed for his academic accomplishments. The radicals prevailed and the second chair was removed.

The Report of the Exterior Evaluation Committee noted that the "most general reaction we have regarding the overall academic thrust and accomplishments of the Department of American Indian Studies . . . is that of frank astonishment at how much the department has managed to accomplish with so little University support. . . .

"The University has been too impervious and unyielding in its expectations that departmental faculty have traditional credentials in order to have job security. . . ."

So ends the second chair.

The third chairman was the choice of the tribal communities and radical students. The third tribal knight in academic clothes was a gentle person with an unusual sense of political balance, but in the end he was not acceptable to the faculties and administrations who decided once more to make the department their personal colonial business. The administration encouraged the third knight to take academic leave.

The Program Planning Committee reported that "three department chairs have come and gone in fairly rapid succession and there is no chair at the moment. Turnover among valued faculty has also apparently been higher in American Indian Studies than in other departments. . . . It is not surprising that the personnel of the department have fluctuated and that morale has suffered. Unless changes of substance are effectuated, American Indian Studies is not likely to improve. . . ."

So ends the third chair.

The fourth chairman of the department was the choice of the colonial administration. He was no knight; rather, he was a demonic warrior, without a vision, mean but mannered. A dark, brooding reservation born mixedblood, who had been an intelligence officer with unusual experiences in covert operations. No one in the department trusted him, and in time few colonialists sought his presence. He was exposed as an agent provocateur and a double informer for a radical tribal organization dedicated to the destruction of white institutions. When this was learned, the students were more supportive, but the administration fired him in less than two weeks. While he was mining information for various organizations, others were informing on him and it was revealed that he was selling drugs in class and offering grades for sex favors in his office.

So ends the fourth chair.

The fifth chairperson was the first woman and the first black person acceptable to the students, the deans, the administration, and the faculties. She was intelligent, not a knight, but a creator, dedicated to forming an ethnic studies department that would bring together faculties and students from various minorities. She was open, honest, and enthusiastic, but too sensitive to survive mean histories, the abuse from white racists and tribal terrorists, doublecrossing administrators with their hands on their pale cocks, and those who told malignant rumors about her sex preferences and experiences. In less than three months she disappeared and was found alone on a shoulderless road possessed with fear and loathing for academic institutions.

So ends the fifth chair.

The sixth chairman was a tall black mixedblood macho homosexual who sold narcotics and flesh. He was hired because he was mean and because he knew how to control people and behavior, and because he was not serious about the department. He told the search committee that he would "do the work that must be done, and, furthermore, brothers and sisters, we need to show the tribal world that some black people are more tribal than tribal people. . . ." Several months before he became chairman he petitioned to be recognized as a mixedblood tribal person, claiming that his great grandmother was "a pure Indian princess, or something, and she was so powerful she even had slaves . . . well, she fooled around with one of those slaves, and here stands me, a mixedblood tribal black with a smooth tongue, brother." His smooth tongue, however, wagged with no effect when federal narcotic agents registered in his courses and busted the proud mixedblood for selling hard drugs during the showing of the film *A Man Called Horse*. The arrest was made while Richard Harris was hooked on the chest on the screen.

So ends the sixth chair.

Captain Shammer, the seventh chairman of the department, is an unknown mixedblood who arrived by bus with a silent blonde, a dead birch tree, and a backpack loaded with vitamins and herbal medicines. His speech gestures are gentle, and he has a pleasant smile. He allows no questions about his past, but he did tell one reporter that his mother was a woman of the cloth and his father was a man of leather.

"We never travel without the sacred tree at our side," said chairman seven. "Trees hold their space in the world; sacred auras do not end when trees are cut."

"Is there more?" asked Ramon.

"More than you know, mister, we bear this sacred tree because of what Black Elk told John Neihardt after the massacre at Wounded Knee." Shammer held the tree with his right hand, the sacred hand, and touched his faithful blonde with his other hand.

"Foolish of me to ask."

"When I look back now from this high hill of my old age, I can still see the butchered women and children laying heaped and scattered all along the crooked gulch," recited chairman seven while his blonde, her face carved deep with emotion, laced her fingers on his arm.

"As plain as when I saw them with eyes still young. And I can see that something else died there in the bloody mud, and was buried in the blizzard. A people's dream died there. It was a beautiful dream. . . . There is no center any longer, and the sacred tree is dead."

"Lighten up, man," snapped the black secretary. "This is no real world man, there never has been a real world here, we all pretend, rehearsals but no drama. Call me now when you need a form done, a press conference, or something personal. Welcome, welcome, now, to nowhere on the eighth floor."

Captain Shammer served as chairman seven for less than three weeks, nineteen days to be exact, the shortest tenure of all the chairs, but in that time he was the most imaginative and made more dramatic decisions than all the past chairs put together.

On his first day as chairman he offered the department for sale to the highest bidder. During the following two weeks he called six more press conferences to announce his decisions. Because of his reputation for unusual and imaginative conference show solutions, or *solucination*, as he called them, to the problems in tribal studies, the number of news organizations increased from two reporters at his first conference, to sixteen reporters, including radio, television, newspapers, and magazines, at his seventh and last conference. And the audience increased from the first event, where he sat on his desk in the converted supplies room, to hundreds in the auditorium. His blonde and his sacred tree were at his sides at all news events.

Captain Shammer announced at his second news conference, on his fourth day as chairman seven, in a calm and pacific voice, that he was ordering star blankets and ribbon shirts for all skins and mixedbloods in the department "so as to distinguish the tribal students and teachers from the rest of the academic world."

"But anyone can wear a ribbon shirt and spread a star blanket," said a reporter. "What's the difference?"

"Mister reporter, it is better that a white man be trapped in a ribbon shirt than a tribal person captured in a dark suit and tie," responded chair seven.

Captain Shammer announced at his third news conference, on his fifth day as chair, that he was establishing a new *Halfbreed Hall of Fame* to celebrate the unusual achievements of those with mixedblood descent.

"Who do you have in mind?"

"Captain Shammer the trickster."

"Anyone else?"

"Bonnie Wallace."

"More."

"Ronald Libertus."

"More."

"Fullblood mixedbloods and mixedblood fullbloods, and all tribal participants, no matter what their handicaps, in the Halfbreed Open Golf Tournament."

"Who are they?"

"Skins in doubleknit red leisure suits, white shoes, and the self-appointed fullbloods who are mixedbloods will be pleased to celebrate their mixed descent if it means a place in the *Mixedblood Hall of Fame*," explained the seventh chair.

"Geometric blood volume was introduced by colonial racists, and from time to time, measure to measure, depending upon the demands of federal programs and subsidies, tribal blood volume increases or decreases. You could say that tribal blood volume follows the economic principles of supply and demand."

"How interesting," said a reporter.

"Bonnie Wallace has given much thought and humor to the blood volume of *indianness*, the over and under *indianness*," chair seven continued, driving his hands deep into his pockets. "She proposed an organization of mixedblood skins which demands one-fourth degree of tribal blood *or less*, to be enrolled as a member. She also advised the Bureau of Indian Affairs to change our *enrollment numbers* to our *surrender numbers*, because we were given numbers in exchange for land and resources."

The audience, including reporters and students, applauded chair seven when he raised his hands to end his third media event. The lights dimmed and the trickster soared from the auditorium with his sacred tree and his blonde laced to his left arm.

Captain Shammer announced at his fourth news conference, on his seventh day as chairman, that he had invited all tribal students in the past decade, those who had received incomplete grades, "to come to a department *incomplete celebration*, during which time all grades of incomplete will be changed to a passing grade." This *incomplete celebration*, first met with humor, turned to horror in the office of the registrar because about eighty percent of all courses that tribal students registered for ended with an incomplete grade. The celebration changed more than three thousand grades, and improved the enrollment statistics for the department. Shammer, on the seventeenth day as chair, was applauded in public as a shaman trickster who expressed more imaginative ideas about higher education than a hundred faculties in future studies.

"Our chairman, the best mixedblood out of six," the students chanted at the *incomplete celebration*, "one, two, three, four, five, six, seven, we want seven to last forever, seven is the shaman chairman, seven lives forever."

Captain Shammer announced at his fifth news conference, on his thirteenth day as chairman, that all "tribal faculties and students would be paid a basic wage according to their volume of tribal blood, as a means of reducing racial discordance, and that all increases in salaries after that would be based on merit, kind trickeries, and good humor."

"What does that mean?"

"Blood reparations," explained chairman seven. "But no one should be advanced from his basic blood wage for racial claims alone; tribal salaries increase with good humor. . . . Suppose, for example, that it was true that Colin Defender was in fact related to a tribal princess, as he has claimed on social occasions, then Slash and Burn would get a small stipend for his princess blood but little more for tribal merit."

Captain Shammer turned pale behind the bank of microphones. The television cameras whirred from otherworlds, and the lights were harsh and cruel on his face. The audience at the fifth news conference filled a large auditorium. Chairman seven looked to his right and held the sacred tree, and to his left he touched his blonde companion. No one had ever heard her speak, but she did smile when she looked at her special shaman.

Behind chairman seven was a large wheel covered with a red velvet throw. He gestured with his head and his blonde attendant pulled the cord which released the velvet cover. Beneath was a large wheel with sixteen wedges of color around the edge. The colors increased in darkness from pale white to pink, light browns, and a dark brown. Corresponding to each wedge of color was a code number. The numbers referred to explanations in a manual on tribal skin tones and identities.

Captain Shammer smiled and waited in silence behind the bank of microphones for someone to ask the obvious question.

"How does the wheel work?"

"Excellent question, sir," responded the chairman, less than sincere. "Permit me now to demonstrate this scientific approach to blood volume, degrees, and quantities of tribalness, and an index of the basic racial wage skin tone."

Shammer stood in front of the wheel, his head in the circle, while his faithful blonde turned the outer edge of the wheel to a wedge that matched his flesh tone.

"The color number is four," explained chairman seven, "and let me read from the fourth chapter of the manual:

"*Four* on the color wheel is a sacred number that corresponds to the moon of the popping trees, and the four directions and dimensions. The positive aspect is balance not dominance, while the negative aspects of four are division and incompletion.

"Mixedbloods with the skin tone color wheel code *four* are too mixed to choose absolute breeds or terminal creeds. Fours are too light to dance in the traditional tribal world and too dark to escape their flesh in the white world. Fours are four color prints, three colors and black, a fine line balance on the drum. Fours dream their corners together.

"Fours bear the potential to be four flushers, too much white in the hand and not enough in the tribal bush. Fours are four bits from the whole moon but make the best balancers under the popping trees."

"Chairman Shammer, permit me this brief preface to a series of questions, sir," said a local newspaper reporter. Writers seldom ask questions while television people are present, because too often their thoughts are broadcast before their stories are published, giving the impression that newspaper writers rewrite television reports, but in this case it was necessary. Chairman seven does not meet with reporters but in public. If a writer asserts his summaries and evaluations before a series of questions, the news figure is inclined to respond in a more personal and specific manner, which, according to the writer who questioned chairman seven, "eliminates the tube freaks because none knows enough to listen."

"Perhaps, sir, we could turn down the hot television lights for my questions," the writer said, nodding to his competition in the rows.

"Yes, of course, nothing but plastic and human mutations could live under these lights in this place," said the seventh chair.

"These lights are so unnatural, even abusive. . . . I have attended all of your conferences, sir, perhaps you remember that I was one of two reporters at your first conference in your office closet, and, in a manner of speaking, we have come out of the closet together. . . ."

The audience hissed.

"Forget the closet histories, sir, my questions are connected to the observation that you are a fool. . . ."

The audience hissed.

"Rather, sir, a special fool, a fool in the best sense of a tribal trickster or shaman, which suggests that you are here to balance the department, perhaps the world. . . ."

The audience applauded.

"Now, we have some ideas about what was the trouble in the past in the department, but what is the trouble now which you seek to balance?"

"What was the past trouble?"

"In a word, incompetence."

"Thank you," said chair seven. "My answer is this: no more incompetent than the deans, but now we seek to balance incompetence with the opposite."

"What is the opposite?"

"Contraries are the difference and nothing but the differences that balance the world . . . the opposite of a dean is nothing more than a trickster and humor, sir," said chair seven.

The audience applauded.

"But how did you know what to balance?" asked the reporter. He was distracted when the television floodlights were switched on for the responses of chairman seven. More distracting, however, and more interesting, was the audience. Conversations were carried on all over the auditorium. People seemed more affectionate and joked about forming a trickster political party.

"Forgive me, sir, I was distracted by the television lights," the writer said as he turned pages in his notebook. "Could you repeat your last remarks."

"Balance is not balance, no idea or event *is* what it is named, there are no places that are known but through the opposites, nothing is sacred but what is not sacred. . . . No thing is in balance but what is confused and in discordance," said Captain Shammer. "The trickster seeks the balance in contraries and the contraries in balance; shaman tricksters avoid the extremes, but not with extreme humor or intense manners."

"Did you leave something out?"

"Yes, the trouble with the department is that it is in a troubled and confused balance, predictable in discordance, and in this case the trickster would balance the imbalanced balance. . . . Tomorrow the rain and thunder comes late in the morning during our news conference, and all the kites and folded paper airplanes will gather on the eighth floor in magical flight . . . know the wind in your head first and then remember the trees."

The audience applauded the seventh chairman when he turned to leave with his tree and his blonde laced to his arm. He paused at the side door and looked back, his glance becalmed the audience.

Later, in recollections and stories, it was told that an aura surrounded him; even his thin reddish moustache seemed to burn with a blue flame. A young mixedblood from the urban reservation said, "his eyes flashed in the dark, and his shoulders moved like a crow, like this . . . " she added, thrusting her chest and her lips forward in the tribal avian manner.

Captain Shammer announced at his sixth news conference, on his fifteenth day as chairman, that Old Darkhorse, founder of the *Half Moon Bay Skin Dip* located in California, would be with the Department of American Indian Studies for one month as a special color consultant.

"Old Darkhorse founded his skin dipper when the darkest mixedbloods were much too critical of the light inventions; the pale skin varieties needed darker flesh to disburden their lack of confidence around white liberals," explained chairman seven.

Captain Shammer asked that the television technicians not turn on the bright floodlights until one of their reporters asks a question, and he is prepared to answer. The reporters sulked, as if their allowances had been reduced, and then one by one, with dramatic emphasis, the lights were turned down.

"What will he do here?"

"Will he teach?"

"Could he be eighth in the chair of tears?"

"Who would be dipped?"

"Old Darkhorse reasoned that in a racist place, where skin color is the first consideration, darker dipped flesh would save the race from the racists. . . .

"Darkhorse has dunked several important national leaders, including one tribal commissioner, two deputies, and at least a dozen pale mixedbloods who were elected to reservation tribal offices. In each case, the dunking improved their relationships with white and tribal people. One dunk can turn the corner for a light-skinned mixedblood, but no one has invented a dip to toughen their skin to politics in general."

Darkhorse tried hundreds of herbs and roots and barks until he found the perfect invented red skin color, but at first, during the trial and error time, when dips were free for the asking, he turned several desperate mixedbloods a marbled tone, like the end papers on old books. Those he dunks now stand with the natural dark skins, and few can tell the real from the dipped, "or one dunk from another."

Shammer was weakened by the television lights which flashed on whenever he paused to speak. He seemed even more pale; the color of the white paper on the sacred birch tree at his right side, ever at his sacred right, was no lighter than his bloodless hands. The flame of his blue aura was imperceptible in the bright lights.

"Did he ever dunk himself?" asked a reporter.

"Are white people invited to the dunk?"

"Have you ever been dunked?"

"What are the chemical dangers?"

"Old Darkhorse and the Shammer trickster have never been dunked, so we do not speak from absolute experiences. Darkhorse, however, has natural dark skin. What he needs is a white dunk. . . . But the reports have all been enthusiastic. Nothing to worry about.

"An albino tribal woman wrote from the reservation, 'if being dark is a drag, I can be white and cool again in two years.' In fact, she alternates, two years dunked dark, and when the dunk fades, one year as a white skin again. She dances on both sides of the square, so to speak.

"The Skin Dip will be opened first to mixedblood skins, and then to white people, who are thrilled with sacred skin games," Captain Shammer explained. He paused and smiled. The audience smiled back.

"Let me braid it together now: The department will be sold, incompletes are dissolved, enrollment leaped too high to count, wages based on skin color will increase with a dunk or two, and we expect thousands of whites, some with high cheekbones and *ancestor* dreams, noble savage romances worn down in the word wars, will dunk dark and come back to the departmental tribe which should turn tribal academics from red to black, or red to brown, or white to red . . . white to red in a four color accounting process."

Captain Shammer held high the trickster energies in his voice, but his body seemed to weaken from the news conferences. When he walked from the stage this time, his silent and faithful blonde directed his course from the auditorium.

Captain Shammer called his seventh and last news conference, on his seventeenth day as chair, to open the sealed bids and to announce the new owner of the department.

Thunder clouds wheeled in from the west. The wind whistled under the window sills and ran wild down the halls to the auditorium where chairman seven, at his seventh and last news conference, was about to open the sealed bids for the sale of the Department of American Indian Studies.

"Seventeen sealed letters were received by the closing date," said chairman seven. "I have them here in my hand." He raised his right hand to show the bundle of sealed letters. The wind whistled, and the television cameras whirred, and the audience applauded the mixedblood tribal show.

"You have been so attentive, and so enthusiastic, at these news conferences. . . . We are pleased, do you think we could earn college credit for our experiences here?"

The audience applauded.

Captain Shammer asked the audience to vote on the best bid, and the audience wheeled approval as loud as a thunderstorm. Shammer then invited four volunteers from the audience to assist him and his faithful blonde in the event.

"Imagine," said chairman seven with a wide blue smile, "offering whole nations for sale back to the people who built them, turn the earth back to the earth.

"While I am opening the bids and recording the information on this overhead projector, the volunteers will pass out blue examination books for you to record your vote for the new owner of the department.

"Remember, there are seventeen sealed bids, consider them all and then vote for one."

Captain Shammer shuffled the bids and then opened the first one on the pile. The bidders were instructed to limit their comments to one short paragraph. The first sealed bid came from the "Short Hair Barber School in What Cheer, Iowa. We offer five hundred dollars cash and a free haircut to all students in the department as long as the trees grow and the rivers flow."

The audience moaned.

Second bid: Magical Flight Genetic Engineers. The future is open to new mutations; we bid one million dollars for the rights to patent superindians altered and developed in our laboratories.

The audience turned savage. Hundreds of people leaped to their feet and condemned research that would alter the natural biological world. It appeared that the second bid would be rejected.

Third bid: Wild Women Bait and Tackle Shop of Park Rapids. For one thousand dollars we will turn the department into the most powerful feminist organization in the world. We are the world, and sister power is mother earth power. Indian men have caused the troubles in the department; we will eliminate the men and restore the department to the creative power of women.

The audence was silent.

Fourth bid: We are not certain but the Committee on Tribal Indecision might make a tentative offer to discuss the accidental formation of a *Department of Undecided Studies.* We have a low-standing record of nonfeasance reversals, and indecision, and, for an unreasonable fee, we could unplan your department, and undecide your curriculum. We have few responses from our late proposals, but with the best-managed Indian time avoidance we have turned academic retentives into unfocused and untroubled departments of undecided studies. We have learned from being late at meetings that most Indians graduate before deciding on their course of studies. There you have it, a natural tribal unit, the *Department of Undecided Studies.*

The audience cheered with wild enthusiasm.

The idea about undecided studies comes from Bonella Wallace, who, while working in higher education, was surprised to find so few people with a decided major. "Undecided studies," said Wallace at an unscheduled meeting, "is as important as Indian time . . . but we will never be sure where to meet or when to attend class or who will teach what in undecided studies. . . . The space committee could never decide where to meet, so no one knows where the *Department of Undecided Studies* is located."

A student found, by chance, an unscheduled course offered by the *Department of Undecided Studies*, but the instructor was not sure which course he was supposed to teach and he was never sure about dates and certain tribal events. For example, he once said in class that a "massacre happened, well, what was the day now, well, choose a date for now, give it five or ten years either way, but don't quote me."

Bonella Wallace explained that other unplanned courses include blood quantum separation, nude welding, cohabitation cures, tribal histories based on humor and rumor, and psychic boarding school curricula, with field displacement at Fort Rotten, Oklahoma.

Fifth bid: DINE Television of Window Rock, Arizona, a subsidiary of the Navajo Nation, bids all costs and supports to build a special tribal television communication school and promotion center, to sell television advertising, with tribal models.

The audience was silent.

Sixth bid: Indian Guides. For more than two decades white fathers and sons have been practicing the sacred roles of the American Indians. We believe that we are now the best-qualified white Indians in the world, with the possible exception of one or two Karl May Indian Clubs in Germany, to rule the Department of American Indian Studies as a warrior society in traditional costumes. We make our own costumes with plastic beads and chicken feathers.

The audience laughed.

Seventh bid: San Francisco Sun Dancers. Got no money but us earthdivers got a good vision, an urban vision to survive in the cities. And one thing is clear, your place needs an urban vision. Let us know how.

The audience was silent.

Eighth bid: Indian inmates at the South Dakota State Penitentiary. We want out, out, out, out, when you sell your place out there could you come down here and sell ours too?

The audience cheered.

Ninth bid: Fine Friends of the Future, Wild West Branch of the National Association of Futurists. Name your price and simulation game. We have never said no to an idea, and we never use conditionals or the future tense in our future tongue. You *will* not hear forked tongue talk with us in the future.

The audience chanted *will, will, will, will.* . . .

Tenth bid: General Custer Retirement Hotel in Roundup, Montana. The trouble with injuns is the wild west got scared out of them. Send some loosers down this way, we know how to nock heads in line, and we wont charge much either.

The audience laughed.

Eleventh bid: Little Ramon, Department of American Indian Studies. I am the secretary of the department, and I think that I should be considered first if the department is sold. I offer two thousand dollars in cash, and I can borrow more. I am the only one who knows how to keep this place in order.

The audience was silent.

Twelfth bid: Cambridge Degrees. The world is peopled with brilliant, intelligent people without college degrees, and we know that most tribal people never complete their college course work because the institution does not recognize their brilliance. We offer all college degrees for a small fee, and we pledge a share of our profits to expand our operation within a real academic department. We consider this a rare opportunity; terms are negotiable. All students will receive a complimentary doctorate degree in a field of their choice. Doctor Peter Fountain is one of ours.

The audience cheered.

Thirteenth bid: My name shall remain unknown. I am a widow with substantial wealth, and I will offer money to help the department survive. It would be a shame to see such a fine idea fail for lack of institutional support.

The audience cheered.

Fourteenth bid: Edge of the Earth Society, Fortuna, North Dakota. Our bid may be different from any others. We assist individuals to make the break and to go over the edge with a good feeling. Our organization has been of service to thousands of satisfied people going over the edge, and we offer to you, and your department, free passes to the edge of the earth and one trip over.

The audience laughed.

Fifteenth bid: The Whole Truth Wholistic Health Institute of Los Angeles. In the ball games of life diets are the home runs. We have helped people change their lives and the world with our Whole Truth diet plans and nutritional products. We will buy the department with good food, and in a few short weeks the teachers and students will be dancing in the halls, between classes of course. You have more to lose in fast foods.

The audience applauded with their lips.

Sixteenth bid: Hubert Humphrey Flash Backers. The Flash Backers are a group of promoters associated with mineral and timber companies interested in the development of natural resources on tribal lands. We are prepared to offer substantial cash, plus bonuses to individuals, and a percentage of the profits. We all could stand to maximize our income, and at the same time serve the needs of a growing nation. As owners of the Department of American Indian Studies we would organize a special academic program in the management of natural resources on tribal lands, and find positions in large firms for the graduates. The sacred mother earth is our best teacher, and she teaches us all, white and tribal, to take what we can when we need it—and what we need is what we take for the economic well-being of the nation.

The audience hissed.

Seventeenth bid: An expert on Indian issues for the *Minneapolis Tribune* offered to buy the department so that he and other reporters would always have a good liberal cause to report when the news was slow.

The audience demanded the removal of the last bid.

"There you have it," said chair seven, wringing his hands like a fly on a grapefruit. "The most unusual seventeen sealed bids. . . . What seems remarkable is that only two bids were connected to higher education, Little Ramon and the Navajo National television station, and only one bid was a statement of open, unencumbered support."

Captain Shammer turned from the microphones; his glance becalmed the audience. The place was silent, but for the wind turning corners and the sound of rain on the tall windows in the back of the auditorium.

"Now it is time to vote," said chair seven in a deep and seductive voice. "Write the name and number of one bidder from the list. Choose the bid that you would accept as the new owner of the department. Write the name in your blue books and then pass them to your right to be gathered by the volunteers."

The writers and reporters at the seventh news conference were asked to count and record the votes. The count took several minutes; people in the audience chatted and told stories. There were special energies in the auditorium, a friendliness and peacefulness, the calm which follows a severe thunderstorm.

Later, when the vote was completed, two students from the audience came forward and dominated the lectern. The students in turn explained their pleasure during the news conferences, the fresh voice and imaginative ideas which are uncommon in higher education, and led the audience to insist that the silent blonde make the announcement of the new owner of the department. The approach was unusual, and chair seven was alerted to the manners of tricksters. "We have never heard her speak, what better time to break the silence than this announcement," said the shorter of the two students. The audience applauded, cheered, and then the auditorium was again silent.

Captain Shammer turned to his left, toward his faithful blonde laced to his arm, and smiled. She moved with her lover to the bank of microphones, and in silence looked around the audience. Hundreds of faces smiled in anticipation when she moved her lips to speak.

Silence.

The reporters handed her the envelope that contained a piece of folded paper with the vote totals. The blonde held the paper with one hand in front of her at the microphones.

Silence.

She unlaced her fingers and opened the folded paper. The sound was amplified over the microphones. She looked around the audience again, her lips moved, faces in the audience smiled back, but she remained silent.

The audience applauded.

The audience knew the owner of the department.

Silence.

"Captain Shaman Shammer," she read, and when she looked up from the paper, people in the audience leaped to their feet, applauding, cheering, whistling, and dancing in the aisles. The audiience ignored the seventeen bids and wrote in their own; the audiience voted for Captain Shammer.

Captain Shammer was overwhelmed, double tricked in a trickster audience, an unexpected celebration, but ownership of the department was the last thing he had in mind, even as a trickster. He smiled and smiled and smiled, but his sense of contraries and spiritual energies were leaving him too fast in the terminal creeds of a crowd. His faithful blonde showed him the paper with the unanimous vote and then laced her hands back on his arm. Chairman seven bowed four times to the audience, superior tricksters, and disappeared, leaving a pale blue aura soaring in the auditorium.

Shammer did not depend on an audience for his energies and good humor, rather, audiences took his energies; he was a shaman trickster who sought his connections to the earth in visions and dreams, not in rehearsals and audiences. Spirits and animals demand their show in dreams, but crowds go for the heart. Their needs consume the mysteries and blood secrets of the earth.

So ends the news conference.

Captain Shammer, on the nineteenth day as chairman, was visiting, his faithful blonde at his side, with Little Ramon and several faculty members in the main roost for no more than five minutes. He announced that he was awarding the department to the Committee on Tribal Indecision and changing the name to the *Department of Undecided Studies*. During the meeting the sacred dead tree was stolen from his storage room office around the corner.

Silence.

Captain Shammer was seen later that morning near the river with his red backpack and his blonde laced to his right arm. No one has heard from him since the morning the sacred dead tree was stolen.

"Department of Undecided Studies," answered Ramon.

"This is Dean Defender," said Slash and Burn, "let me talk to the new chair, Captain Shammer." His call came three weeks after the disappearance of the seventh chair. The tribal chair was the real chair of tears.

"Shammer is gone," said Ramon.

"Who do we have in the hopper now, little tiger?" asked Slash and Burn. "Were there ever *real* savages in the world, whatever were the settlers worried about?"

"Indecision."

"Indians are best as great grandmothers," said Slash and Burn. "This new breed came out of the woodwork and were worn out on the concrete."

"So turns the tribal world."

"Shammer missed a lunch date in the Faculty Club," said Dean Colin Defender. "We will never know what he had in mind for the department."

So ends the seventh chair.

Love

Born to Lose

BLOODLINE TRIBAL SURVIVORS

Sand Creek Survivors

> In the national experience race has always been of greater importance than class. . . . Racism defined natives as nonpersons within the settlement culture and was in a real sense the enabling experience of the rising American empire: Indian-hating identified the dark others that white settlers were not and must not under any circumstances become, and it helped them wrest a continent and more from the hands of these native caretakers of the lands.
>
> Richard Drinnon, *Facing West*

First Lieutenant James Cannon testified at the hearing on the Sand Creek Massacre that the tribal bodies he saw after the attack were scalped and butchered by federal troops, "and in many instances their bodies were mutilated in the most horrible manner. . . . I heard of one instance of a child a few months old being thrown in the feed box of a wagon, and after being carried some distance, left on the ground to perish. I also heard of numerous instances in which men had cut out the private parts of females, and stretched them over the saddle bows, and wore them over their hats, while riding in the ranks."

Dane Michael White buckled his wide belt around his thin neck and hanged himself from a shower rod in the Wilkin County Jail in Breckenridge, Minnesota. Dane had been held in jail as a criminal for forty-one days, most of that time alone, in isolation, the victim of dominant white colonial institutions. A tribal child with short hair and wide smile, a survivor from Sand Creek, dead at thirteen. Suicide.

Dane White and the Sand Creek Massacre in Colorado are three generations apart in calendar time, but in dreams and visual tribal memories, these grievous events, and thousands more from the White Earth Reservation to the damp concrete bunkers beneath the interstates in San Francisco, are not separated in linear time. The past can be found on tribal faces in the present. The curse of racism rules the ruinous institutions and federal exclaves where tribal people are contained; where tribal blood is measured on colonial reservations. Dane White became a criminal for being truant from a white school.

Clement Beaulieu, mixedblood writer and college teacher, was on special assignment for the *Minneapolis Tribune* at the Red Lake Reservation. For official purposes he was compiling background information on reservation economic development. His personal reasons, however, were tied to tribal friends and his need to hear some fine stories.

Beaulieu had settled into stories and imaginative memories, like an old reservation mongrel, when he was called to the telephone by Frank Premack, the city editor of the *Minneapolis Tribune*, and ordered to be in Sisseton, South Dakota, by morning for a funeral.

"Premack, your humor is cruel," Beaulieu responded long distance. "Sisseton is more than two hundred miles from here."

"Be there."

"But I've been drinking, I'm tired, and I would have to drive all night, alone," Beaulieu pleaded. "The truth is, the best stories are just starting here, good reservations stories. . . . Who is so damned important that we have to cover a funeral in Sisseton?"

"Dane Michael White."

"Who is he?"

"An Indian suicide."

Silence.

"His father lives in Browns Valley, and his mother was living in Chicago, but she moved back to Sisseton. Dane was held in jail like a fucking criminal for forty-one goddamned days . . . cover the funeral, telephone me from there, I want a front page story."

Premack was one of the toughest journalists, perhaps the meanest at times, but he was also one of the most sensitive editors at the *Minneapolis Tribune*. No doubt that he was the most imaginative, the most demanding, and the hardest-working editor. Few writers could keep up with him; he caused revolutions in individual writers and readers. His writers loved him and hated him at the same time. When he was a writer, he was so critical of malfeasance and so perceptive of nonfeasance in government that when he was promoted to editor, elected officials celebrated the departure of his questions and his reports on city government.

"Have a nice drive."

"Shit. . . ."

Beaulieu drank three cups of coffee and started driving at midnight, south through Bemidji, Park Rapids, while whistling in the dark and listening to radio music from Chicago and Little Rock.

The world comes together all at once, he wrote in his notes, when time is turned loose like an animal in the mind park.

Dane White at Sand Creek. Tribal worlds converged between Detroit Lakes and Fergus Falls. Beaulieu thrust his head out the window into the cold wind. Late November, no snow, the earth was tired. Tribal worlds converged in imagination and individual memories. Ceremonial words seemed to bend down on the shoulder of the road, but no one would wait to listen. Even the earthdivers soared past the last tribal survivors through the dark in dreams.

"Dane White is here, in the background of the banquet table," Father William Keohane said in prayer. His gestures were solemn; in slow and tedious motions, his arms and shoulders turned like the branches on an ornamental fruit tree, turning on the wind toward the large painting of the Last Supper mounted like a fastfood billboard behind the small altar in the narrow church. "Lord, remember this child in your Kingdom."

Beaulieu listened. *Remember this child*, turned in his mind over and over like a phrase that never found a place to fit in time. *When is the best time to remember?* Trained to be a dutiful scribe, at least as a reporter, he scratched into his notebook the practiced gentle words of the priest, but he resisted the words, his hand seemed to avoid the words, he hated the words. The sounds burst in his ears and shot down his arm, nothing smooth or soothing, nothing from forgiveness, no calm, no peace from tribal suicide.

How can his words be so soft, so restrained, Beaulieu wrote in his notes. Dane knows no pleasure in the words of the white world; he was trapped and executed in a white institution . . . and now the apologists mutilate this child with funeral words, in the same place in the tribal heart where tribal children were tossed on bayonets and women were dismembered by savage white soldiers. . . . The white apologists repress the revolutions in the heart. . . . Lord, remember what the soldiers and the white world have done to the caretakers of this land.

Clement Beaulieu stepped into a telephone booth to call Frank Premack, his editor. The door was broken, the small space smelled of urine and cigarette smoke. The wind snarled through the cracks in the booth.

"Sisseton is tired."

"I want photographs," said Premack.

"No camera."

"Buy a cheap one at the drugstore, somewhere, and airfreight the film to me this afternoon. . . . We can process it before the last edition. This is front page; send me several shots from the grave."

"Have you ever been out here?"

"Yes, I lived in Aberdeen."

"Well, then you know too well."

"Know what?"

"Cold wind and no fresh fruit."

"Repression, repression can best be measured in the world by the availability of fresh fruit and vegetables," said the editor. "Give me a minute to write that down."

"I am tired."

"We all are, forget it."

"No, these prairie prisons exhaust me."

"Forget the women."

"I was not thinking about women."

"Forget your ideals."

"No, it is the heart that suffers out here."

Saint Catherine's Indian Mission Church hunkered like a trained circus animal in the center of little unpainted houses too close together in double rows; each tied to concrete ribbons. The Indian

Mission was dressed in gentle colors, pastel blue and pink, visual denials of violence and internal revolutions. The sidewalk and steps had been washed and swept clean for the funeral. Tribal people arrived in bright red and blue cars, dressed in dark church clothes, men in doubleknit suits and blue shoes, and women dressed in white shoes and print dresses. The cold wind whipped their dresses, shivers ran down their bare arms to the mission door. The prairie wind pushed at the door, holding it closed. A tribal spiritual wind.

Inside the chapel the wind had taken up with the sweet smell of flowers. The metal coffin was closed, locked, institutional isolation, the neck bruises hidden from view, locked from memories. The wooden benches were hard; the service was proper, dull, and repressed in pale colors. Pink and blue sacred auras abounded on the walls, painted with exaggerated bows, white saints who must have soared with the settlers.

We should pull these words down, beat them on the altars until the truth is revealed, beat the sweet phrases from the institutions that have disguised the horrors of racism . . . drive the word pains and agonies from the heart into the cold. . . . We are the victims of these words used to cover the political violence and white horrors in the memories of the tribes.

Hear these primal screams, the tribes scream with the trees and rivers, from diseases, the massacres and mutilations of the heart. . . . racist isolation and the repression of the heart in white schools and institutions. . . . Break down the white word walls and dance free from isolation . . . dance in the sun.

The procession to the grave was slow and tedious, a mechanical ritual of fifteen automobiles. Even the raw earth, the real earth from beneath the frost line, was covered with an unnatural green carpet, brighter than the prairie burial site. Funerals are for the living, but the tribes were buried in the heart, silent, alone, repressed. Those at the grave seemed to be the last survivors of white racism.

The tribal procession wobbled over the stubble in the cold wind . . . circling the bodies from memories at Sand Creek and Marias River and Wounded Knee we bear the new tribal dead in metal tubs locked to keep death a secret and locked to keep the earth from our bones that reach back to the earth . . . back to our tribal graves.

Hands in white gloves reached to cover an occasional smile, but the eyes, dark tribal eyes, smiled wide over the hidden lips and uneven teeth in the line. There was an innocence and a sense that the innocent were the new victims.

The Blackfeet were sleeping in their village on the Marias River. It was January, cold and dark. The commanding officers ordered the soldiers to "aim to kill, to spare none of the enemy. . . . A terrible scene ensued." This report was published in *Survey of Conditions of Indians in the United States*, and reprinted in *Of Utmost Good Faith* by Vine Deloria.

"Bears Head, frantically waving a paper which bore testimony to his good character and friendliness to the white man, ran toward the command on the bluff, shouting to them to cease firing, entreating them to save the women and children; down he also went with several bullet holes in his body. Of the more than four hundred souls in camp at that time, very few escaped. And when it was over, when the last wounded woman and child had been put out of misery, the soldiers piled the corpses on overturned lodges, firewood, and household property and set fire to it all. . . . Several years afterward I was on the ground. Everywhere scattered about in the long grass and brush, just where the wolves and foxes had left them, gleamed the skulls and bones of those who had been so ruthlessly slaughtered. . . ."

According to G. B. Grinnell, "innocent persons were butchered on this day of shame, ninety of them women, fifty-five babies . . . no punishment of any kind was given the monsters who did it."

American Horse, a survivor at Wounded Knee, testified that "right near the flag of truce a mother was shot down with her infant; the child not knowing its mother was dead was still nursing, and that was especially a very sad sight. The women as they were fleeing with their babes on their backs were killed together, shot right through and women who were heavy with child were also killed. . . .

"Little boys who were not wounded came out of their places of refuge, and as soon as they came in sight a number of soldiers surrounded them and butchered them there."

At the end, when the metal coffin was lowered into the sacred prairie, the six pallbearers, relatives and tribal friends, removed their honoring ribbons from their new suits and dropped them into the grave in silence.

Dane Michael White was buried in an isolated grave, but he must not be forgotten. He must soar in memories with millions of tribal people from the past, their faces in the sun, their smiles in the aspen, their death and our memories a revolution in the heart. We are dancing in the sun . . . we are the pallbearers and the ghost dancers.

"This is Premack."

"Who is taking dictation?"

"Keep it short," said the editor who typed with two fingers and ground his teeth between spoken words. "The second coming is worth no more than a page and a half."

Clement Beaulieu was standing in the telephone booth with the broken door. The prairie wind whipped through the narrow space. He opened his notebook and dictated his story about the funeral.

"First paragraph: Traditional white colonial racists banished tribal cultures and isolated the survivors. . . ."

"Save it for the archives," said Premack.

"What *is* the news?"

"Start dictating," said Premack, grinding his teeth.

"November 21, 1968, dateline Sisseton.

"Catholic funeral services for Dane Michael White were held here Wednesday in English and in the Dakota language at St. Catherine's Indian Mission Church. New paragraph.

"Following the service, attended by seventy-five people, all but six of whom were Dakota Indians, Dane was buried in St. Peter's Catholic Cemetery. New paragraph.

jail," said the attorney. "I had been told that placing Dane with his grandmother, Marion Starr, had already been decided." There is no record that the court-appointed attorney visited his client or grandmother; rather, he postponed the next scheduled hearing to prepare for the case.

Dane could have been placed in the Pierre Indian Boarding School in South Dakota. School administrators indicated that there was space, but juvenile court officials could not decide on a date to discuss the matter.

Meanwhile, Dane White was alone in a civilized world with little more in a white institution than his tribal dreams. He lettered the word "love" on the back of his belt and wrote "born to lose" on his tennis shoes.

I looked down upon the earth and saw a flame which looked to be a man. . . . I heard all around voices of moaning and woe, Black Elk told John Neihardt in an interview. *It was sad on earth. I felt uneasy and I trembled . . . the man transformed into a gopher and it stood up on its hind legs and turned around. Then this gopher transformed into a herb. This was the most powerful herb. . . . It could be used in war and could destroy a nation.*

"Cyrus came in here and said he wanted me to pick him up," Mundt announced, with his feet racked one over the other on his square desk. He was a person of verbal and visual force, expressing few uncertainties on the prairie between the pale marketplace economics and the defeated tribes.

"I asked Sheriff Mundt to pick him up and give him a good scare," said Cyrus White, leaning on his bare elbows over the kitchen table. "Dane was never in school," he explained, "the kids teased him, calling him dumb and stupid. . . . Sheriff Schmitz said he wanted to take Dane to Breckenridge and decided from there what to do with him."

Minnesota Attorney General Douglas Head ordered an investigation of the suicide. According to the official report Dane Michael White was of average intelligence and seemed to have an interest in drawing.

"Dane saw no one on any regular basis," the report concludes, "other than the Wilkin County Sheriff and his wife, who delivered meals to the boy's cell."

Dane shared a cell block with two other boys for four days, but the rest of the time he was alone, in isolation. Dane showed the two boys how he could hang himself, his suicide game, from a shower curtain rod in his cell.

"Dane was visited by members of his family twice, once for less than an hour by his father and once by his stepmother for about half an hour," the official report continues.

"Without a more exhaustive study of how juveniles are treated in the . . . area, it is impossible to say conclusively that this excessively long jailing was because Dane was an Indian.

"However, the fact of his being Indian cannot be dismissed as immaterial. . . . Dane himself never complained and never indicated that he was other than content in jail, except to the boys who shared his cellblock.

"Dane never initiated conversation, but always had a smile for the sheriff and his wife. It was not unlikely that Dane was acting out how he had been taught, as an Indian, to act in front of white persons in authority.

"From our investigation we received the impression that some persons assumed that the jail was superior to Dane's own home. . . . Dane's appearance of contentment undoubtedly promoted some indifference to his continued incarceration."

"This is Premack."

"Premack, listen," said Beaulieu from the telephone booth at the corner, "three stories in four days, I think I'll come back to the office and write about politicians and their apologies for violence and suicide."

"Who postponed the juvenile court hearings?"

"The judge."

"Why?"

"He was on a hunting trip."

"A hunting trip?"

"Big game hunting in the mountains."

"The bastards," said Premack.

"The white man smacks his law and order on the land, possesses the earth until it can hardly breathe, and then he goes hunting in the mountains while the tribes die in his institutions, in cold isolated cells," said Beaulieu, looking down the main street and kicking the side of the telephone booth with his left foot. "Listen, the state investigators for the Attorney General are down here now, and the word is out not to talk to reporters. The politicians want the story for their uses now, everything is useful to a politician. . . . Someone will apologize and look good when he promises that this will never happen again.

"Shit, I can no longer tell who is more violent, politicians or federal troops. More investigations and reports to reduce all the problems to words and conversations with constituents. . . . Politicians are still keeping the world safe with words rather than guns for white settlers."

"Then, what are you doing?"

"Newspaper side shows in the word wars."

"All the more fun. . . ."

"Come the revolution," said Beaulieu.

"Come the next election, remember democracies?"

"The whole damn country is a wild west show."

"Drive with care."

Senator Walter Mondale from Minnesota, acting chairman, after the assassination of Senator Robert Kennedy, of the subcommittee on Indian Education, attributed the suicide of Dane White and other young tribal people to an "identity crisis" resulting from educational experiences "depicting the Indian as a pagan savage. . . .

"Indians find themselves alienated from their own culture. . . . The problems are particularly pronounced in boarding schools where children are separated from parents and community and sometimes discouraged from even visiting their parents," said Mondale, clear and practiced, in a telephone conversation.

Senator Mondale said that one witness at the subcommittee hearings testified that in one jail near the Navajo Reservation, "in a single year three Indian youths hanged themselves from the same water pipe in the same cell."

Senator Robert Kennedy, who formed and was chairman of the subcommittee, "had spent some time with one of the youths who hanged himself, and I was told that the experience had a lasting impact on Senator Kennedy."

Dane Michael White was a survivor from Sand Creek, Baker Massacre at Marias River, Wounded Knee, and hundreds of racial contests on the prairie, and in words he was abandoned at all the cruel crossroads in the white world. Dane was a victim of colonial domination, manipulation, and cultural invalidation, isolation in a white world of peaceful pretensions.

Colonel John Chivington returned to "his old home in Ohio and settled on a small farm. . . . A few years later his house was burned," writes Jacob Piatt Dunn in his book *Massacres of the Mountains; A History of the Indian Wars of the Far West.* Chivington was nominated as a candidate for representative to the legislature, but he "withdrew from the race." About the same time, while he was involved in a bitter disagreement over Indians with Quakers in the Society of Friends, he was pleased to be invited to address a meeting of old settlers in Colorado.

"Whatsays the dust of the two hundred and eight men, women, and children, ranchers, emigrants, herders, and soldiers," said Chivington to an enthusiastic audience of settlers, "who lost their lives at the hands of these Indians? Peaceable? Now we are peaceably disposed, but decline giving such testimonials of our peaceful proclivities, and I say here as I said in my own town, in the Quaker county of Clinton, State of Ohio, one night last week, *I stand by Sand Creek.*"

"The treatment of women, by any Indians, is usually bad, but by the plains Indians especially so," writes Dunn, who was sympathetic to Chivington.

Dunn writes sensational stories about the experiences of white women who were captured by the tribes. "When a woman is captured by a war-party she is the common property of all of them, each night, till they reach their village, when she becomes the special property of her individual captor, who may sell or gamble her away when he likes. . . . She is also beaten, mutilated, or even killed, for resistance. . . ."

Dunn quoted from an article in the *Rocky Mountain News* on the meeting of the settlers and Colonel Chivington. His *speech was received with an applause from every pioneer which indicated that they, to a man, heartily approved the course of the colonel twenty years ago, in the famous affair in which many of them took part, and the man who applied the scalpel to the ulcer . . . in those critical times, was beyond a doubt the hero of the hour.*

"This is the simple truth," writes Dunn. "Colorado stands by Sand Creek, and Colonel Chivington soon afterwards brought his family to the Queen City of the Plains, where his remaining days may be passed in peace.

"What an eventful history! And how, through it all, his sturdy manhood has been manifest in every action. Through all the denunciation of that Indian fight, he has never wavered or trembled. *Others have dodged and apologized and crawled, but Chivington never.*"

Dane Michael White was a survivor waiting to dance in the sun, waiting for the ghost dance and the new world, even in words, and he was a victim who turned his revolution inward to his own end. He died in isolation, sacrificed in a white institution, separated from the mountains and the prairie wind he knew on his walks alone, but he is not now separated from our memories and the memories of the tribal "caretakers of the lands."

Retake on Colonialism

The Indian Rights Association . . . irrespective of party or creed . . . aims to secure the civilization and legal protection of the Indians. . . . This Association would have the Government adopt toward the Indian a policy wise, firm, and continuous, neither capricious nor vacillating, cruel nor sentimental. It recognizes the agency and reservation system only as a temporary expedient, which must in time be completely abandoned as the Indian shall be fitted by practical training to take his place among the whites, and to earn his bread by his own labor. . . . The Association is in hearty sympathy with the general policy advanced by the Indian Bureau, and the efforts exerted by it for the education and civilization of the Indians.

Indian Rights Association, 1884

The Conference on Indian Tribes and Treaties was convened on April 23, 1955, at the University of Minnesota. Julius Nolte, Dean of Extension, welcomed faculties and participants, which included public officials, anthropologists, and tribal representatives from various reservations. Helen Parker Mudgett, Assistant Professor, organized, recorded, and published a transcript of the reports and discussions on the current interpretations of tribal rights and treaties.

"I firmly believe the Indian people have been the forgotten people for many years while other groups have been vocal, and some of us who are not minority people have been quite vocal. . . ." said Miles Lord, Attorney General, State of Minnesota, the first speaker at the conference.

"From my personal experience, when I was an assistant United States district attorney, I was, in effect the county attorney for the Indian reservations and, in prosecuting and handling the matters involving criminal violations for the federal government, I was able to see some of the terrible inconsistencies and inequities which existed as between colored people and other groups; and I was able also to see the same inconsistencies between the Indians and the whites. I believe that we are about twenty years, at least, behind in this particular field."

Lord was the first speaker at the treaties conference, and then he rushed back to the legislature for more important business. Helen Mudgett followed with the introductions of unexpected tribal delegations from various states: Moses Two Bulls, Ben Chief, Bill Fire Thunder, from the Pine Ridge Reservation; Robert Burnette, President of the Rosebud Sioux Tribal Council, and others stood to be recognized in the crowded conference room in the Center for Continuation Study at the University of Minnesota.

The distance in time, time in the oral traditional sense of visions, experiences, and memories, between the tribal participants and the curious new white missionaries must have been too boundless to measure in academic tense. The tribal people there were the survivors, the current victims of colonial abusement, and the white people there, caught in causes and effects, were the liberal heirs to the crimes of an exploitive world view and dominant national pride. The dominant interpretation of federal treaties is no more humane than a medical doctor withholding treatment, depriving the patient of all but data and information about a chronic disease. The rationalizations, the masks and cages, for institutional racism are more depraved than obvious racial exclusiveness. Notwithstanding evil in the world, tribal people find humor, pretend, and prevail, from conference to conference, from treaties to treaties.

"I think it might be well to say just a word or two about the program and why it is being held. . . ." said Julius Nolte. "We have noticed one significant thing, we think, in all of the contacts which we have had with Indians and with the governmental representatives who are in contact with Indians in our state. We suspect that this condition that I am about to comment upon is rather general over the United States and that is, that there is a great deal of confusion as to the legal aspects of the relationship of Indians and whites. This confusion . . . is the diversity that exists in the kind of treaties and agreements that have been made by the United States with different tribes. There have been interpretations, not only of the treaties themselves, but of statutes that have been passed pursuant to the treaties . . . which have been diverse and conflicting. Some of that conflict seems to have arisen out of differences in terms of the treaties themselves; some I think has arisen because of the fact that both whites and Indians have . . . assumed that the same treaty situation exists with respect to other agreements that have been made between the Indians and the whites. Just from that standpoint alone, there is a great confusion in the law. . . .

"But, the sources of confusion, I believe, go somewhat beyond the mere verbal misinterpretations that I have been speaking about and this further source of confusion is not an easy matter for anyone to explain even with the aid of the best legal minds in our country. . . .

"In other words, besides the difference of opinion as to what the treaties contained, there is in our own American law, a serious difference of opinion as to exactly what these treaties were. . . .

"Well, I have indicated that there is confusion, and I am sure that with respect to some of these subjects, there are many views as to what *is* the truth and what *are* the facts. So, the best that the University could do under the circumstances was to try to assemble here a group of people who, because of their familiarity with this type of subject matter—these problems—have opinions founded upon their research and their experience which are worth listening to.

"We hope that you will join with us in trying to do just that: to try to analyze as dispassionately, as tolerantly, as patiently as possible, the fact situations which underlie the relationship of the Indians, as a part of the American people, to the rest of the society. I am sure that the experts will try, as far as they are able, to communicate their ideas with respect to these very important subjects. . . . I can only express the hope that the discussion will be as concise as possible. Conciseness means thoroughness and lucidity. I think that it will also, in connection with this meeting, have to mean, to some extent at least, brevity because it was impossible for us to have this conference except on a weekend because of the fact that many persons whom we wished to have here could come only at that time. We regret the necessity of having to invade the Sabbath for that reason, but we have a feeling that there is no subject which in a sense comes closer to the elements of religious observance than the type of subject matter that we are discussing together in these two days.

"At any rate, the length of time in which we have to go through this material, these facts, is such that I hope all of the discussions may be rather brief and that you will understand the necessity for that because of the time-scheme. I am sure that among those who are here as experts, there will be many who will not agree with all that is said by their colleagues."

The University of Minnesota, of course, "makes no attempt to guarantee any uniformity of opinion. In fact, in the search for truth, as I am sure everyone realizes, it is quite as important to have the differences of opinion brought out—and differences of facts if there is a conflict of evidence—as it is to attempt any explanation of what is before a group that is studying a subject as we are trying to do here in these two days. The University takes no responsibility either for the opinions of those who are here before you or for any uniformity in their opinions. In fact, we hope that we will disagree and through a disagreement, there will be an opportunity for the kind of discussion from which you can all profit. I do hope, though, that if these conflicts of opinion do arise, that the discussion upon them may be held within time-bounds which will let us, at least in some degree, get through our program."

Law Professor Robert McClure, who had volunteered as a photographer, cleared his throat, looked around the room, and then reminded those at the conference that the morning program would "deal specifically with treaties and laws that directly affect the Minnesota Chippewa."

Outside, students hurried past the windows between classes, and the trees were ripe with the first pale green leaves of the season. Farther north, on the reservations, ice could still be found in windless and shaded places.

Our speaker this morning is John Killen, former newspaper reporter, now a law student who has studied treaties, and a "member of the *Minnesota Law Review* which is a publication devoted to matters of legal significance," said Robert McClure with obvious pride.

Treaties with the Minnesota Chippewa:

"The more I examined these treaties," said John Killen, "the more I came to the realization that the problem of the treaties, the laws, and the decisions of the Minnesota Supreme Court and of the United States Supreme Court in connection with these treaties will require at least many years of study to try to determine exactly what the attitude should be, what the attitude has been, and what it will continue to be. So, all I can do today is to examine with you some of these treaties, to show you what they contain, to show what the Court has done with them and to raise problems in connection with these treaties—problems that are going to have to be solved because the entire area of the relations of the federal government and the state government with the Indians is based first of all on these treaties. . . .

"Today, by statute, the Secretary of the Interior has supervision over public business related to Indians and the Commissioner has supervision over the management of all Indian affairs and matters arising out of Indian regulations. He is under the direction of the Secretary of the Interior. But, it should be noted that federal jurisdiction goes back further. . . .

As Dean Julius Nolte pointed out in his presentation this morning, said John Killen, "until the year 1871, the relations with the tribes and bands of the American Indians were created or established by treaty. Then, in 1871, Congress decided that this was not the correct approach. There was a political factor involved here which was that the House of Representatives had the feeling that it did not wish to leave to the Senate alone the right to determine and control what these treaties were going to contain and what they were intended to do. . . . Under the Constitution, treaties require only the approval of the Senate for passage.

"So, in 1871, by act of Congress, treaties could no longer be made with the Indian tribes. The act declared that treaties made before would be honored and would continue in effect. Subsequent arrangements with the Indians were to take the form of agreements between federal government officials on the one hand and the various Indian bands on the other. These agreements were then to be incorporated into a bill and submitted to Congress like any other projected legislation."

The first important treaty that affected the "Minnesota Chippewa was in 1837 when the Chippewa Nation gave up to the United States the territory between the St. Croix and Mississippi Rivers. This treaty was based on the 1825 Sioux-Chippewa boundary line," which, more or less, divides the state from east to west.

"Is there any difference in the attitude taken toward Indian sovereignty over the land in the two treaties?" asked Alexander Lesser, director of the Association of American Indian Affairs, which is located in New York.

"In the 1825 Treaty," Killen responded, "the United States recognized the boundaries as agreed upon in the pre-treaty council. . . . As I was saying, the 1837 Treaty surrendered a large area of land between the St. Croix and the Mississippi. In consideration for this cession, the government agreed to pay for twenty years, $9500 in currency; $19,000 in goods; $3000 to build blacksmith shops and to support the smiths and supply them with iron and steel; $1000 for the farmers for seed and grain; $2000 for food and $5000 in tobacco.

"These payments were to be made every year. Now often, you are going to find inconsistencies within the treaties themselves. . . . Such inconsistencies, in many cases, are providing the bases for Chippewa claims before the Claims Commission.

"The final article which I shall talk about here grants to the Chippewa Nation the right to hunt, fish, and gather wild rice on the lakes, rivers, and lands of the ceded territory during the pleasure of the President of the United States. . . .

"In 1847, there were two further treaties: one which resulted in the surrender of a large land area in central Minnesota by the Chippewa of the Mississippi and Lake Superior; and the other treaty involved a surrender immediately to the west by the Pillager Band," John Killen explained.

"As you can see the treaties up to this point . . . resulted in the surrender only of land, and in a promise on the part of the United

States to pay in goods, or in cash, for this ceded land. Now, the problem of the claims before the federal government on behalf of the Chippewa Nation is an extremely complex problem, as you all know. Many of the bands represented here have claims pending before the Claims Commission.

"In 1854, in the next key-treaty, the Chippewa of Lake Superior gave up a huge triangle which extended from the Canadian border along the shore of Lake Superior and southward to where it met the 1837 treaty-cession line. Its western boundary was . . . set by the Swan and Vermilion Rivers. From this ceded land, the United States set apart the first Minnesota Chippewa reservations —Grand Portage and Fond du Lac. This treaty also makes the differentiation between the Chippewa of Lake Superior and the Chippewa of the Mississippi a matter of official record and brings about a mutual relinquishment of any claim to lands lying east or west . . . of the 1854 treaty-cession line. Furthermore, the Chippewa of the Mississippi agreed that all payments made in conformance with this treaty should be paid to the Chippewa of Lake Superior alone. . . .

"The next great land surrender took place through the Treaty of 1855 with the Chippewa of the Mississippi and the Pillager and Winnibigoshish Bands. By it, they ceded to the United States the great tract of land in central Minnesota which extended roughly from the Swan River to the Red River and from the mouth of the Crow River to the Rainy River in the north. Through this 1855 Treaty, the Mississippi Bands were given reservations on Mille Lacs, Rabbit Lake, Gull Lake, Sandy Lake, Rice Lake, and Lake Pokegama. The Pillager and Winnibigoshish Bands got areas on Cass Lake, Leech Lake, and Lake Winnibigoshish. Of these, the Rice Lake reservation was never, in fact, established because it fell within the area of the Sandy Lake Reservation.

"Now, these reservations in 1855 were set up in the same way as in the 1854 Treaty. The Indians surrendered all of this land to the federal government, including that on which their reservations were to be located. Then, from the federal government back to the Indians came the creation of these land areas to be set apart as reservations. The 1855 Treaty also provided that the President *could* assign up to eighty acres to each head of a family, or person over twenty-one, and that such land could be patented, and would remain exempt from 'taxation, levy, sale or forfeiture' and not subject to alienation or more than a two-year lease until otherwise provided by the state, with the assent of Congress.

"The mixedbloods who were heads of families and resided in the ceded area, outside the reservation boundaries, were to receive eighty acres in fee . . . clear ownership. Again, there was a long list of payments, both in cash and in goods to the tribes and the chiefs which is too long to recite. . . ."

John Killen continued his lecture on treaties: "Other provisions of this treaty extended the liquor ban to the entire ceded area and granted rights-of-way for roads and highways, and pledged the Indians to submit inter-tribal disputes to the President and to obey his decision, as well as to live peacefully among themselves.

"The 1855 Treaty with the Chippewa of the Mississippi lasted only until 1863. In that year, another treaty was made by which the Mississippi Bands agreed, along with the Pillagers and Lake Winnibigoshish group, to give up Mille Lacs, Rabbit Lake, Gull Lake, Sandy Lake, and Lake Pokegama Reservations for a single reservation surrounding three reservations occupied by the Pillagers and others at Cass Lake, Leech Lake and Lake Winnibigoshish.

"Now, the aim of this 1863 Treaty was to consolidate all of the bands at Leech Lake. It might be said that from this 1863 Treaty resulted today what we now call, or can call, the Greater Leech Lake Reservation. The Indians themselves opposed this consolidation. They did not want to move into the reservations created earlier; they did not want to move from their present land. They stayed put and waited for the federal government to act. Because of this refusal on the part of the Chippewa to move to Leech Lake, the federal government, only a year later, made another treaty with the Mississippi Bands. This treaty permitted them to stay on their old reservations until three hundred acres of land were cleared and prepared for planting. The treaty also added a large piece of land extending north approximately to Red Lake Reservation from what we call the Greater Leech Lake Reservation. Furthermore, in this treaty of 1864, the Mille Lacs Band was expressly exempted from the provision and not required to move to the Greater Leech Lake Reservation."

John Killen paused for a moment and then, following an explanation of the exception of the Bois Fort Band, continued discussing the consolidation attempt of 1864 with the Mississippi Bands: "few of them accepted this offer so, in 1867, the government negotiated a new treaty with the Mississippi Bands. In it, they gave up their rights to all of the 1864 reservations areas, except for a large area adjoining Cass Lake, Leech Lake, and Lake Winnibigoshish Reservations. For this, the Indians were to get an additional tract of thirty townships, including White Earth and Rice Lakes. This was the beginning of what today is the White Earth Reservation. The Indians were promised a sawmill, a gristmill, a schoolhouse and free schooling for ten years.

"The land was to be allotted in an interesting way: as soon as an Indian had ten acres under cultivation, he would receive a certificate for forty acres; as soon as he had another ten acres in cultivation, another certificate for forty, until he had certificates for the maximum under the treaty, one hundred sixty acres. The treaty also provided that the land would be exempt from taxation and sale for debt; it could be sold only with the approval of the Secretary of the Interior and then only to another member of the tribe.

"A further treaty provision set out that *in case of the commission by any of the said Indians of crimes against life or property, the person charged with such crimes may be arrested, upon demand of the agent, by the sheriff of the county in which said reservation may be located, and when so arrested may be tried, and if convicted, punished in the same manner as if he were not a member of an Indian tribe.* This seems to have never been enforced in any way.

"It was the intention of the federal government that all Chippewa of the Mississippi would be settled at White Earth and give up all other reservation areas, but the move to White Earth continued to be slow, although at the time, the White Earth area contained approximately eight hundred thousand acres which was enough, according to the calculations, to provide one hundred and sixty acres for every Chippewa family in the state.

"In 1886, after Congress had declared that treaties could no longer be made with Indian tribes, Congress authorized negotiations with the Minnesota Chippewa to bring about this move to

White Earth for all but the Red Lake and Pembina Bands. The Commission appointed pursuant to that resolution secured the consent of a majority of all but the Mille Lacs Reservation. However, they did not visit the Grand Portage Reservation to discuss this move; and when they met with the Fond du Lac Band, they found that they were doing so well on their own that the Commission did not advise them to make the move to White Earth. These agreements were signed, plus another one with the Red Lake Band, by which they would cede two of their three million acres, which land the government would then sell for them. The remaining land was also to be ceded to the United States who would hold it in trust for the Indians. These agreements, however, were never approved by Congress and died without becoming effective. . . ."

"I spoke earlier of the 1886 agreements which were never confirmed and, therefore, never operative. These agreements had been submitted to Congress in December 1886. Early the following February, Congress passed the Dawes, or General Allotment, Act. This authorized the President to establish reservation Indians on allotted lands which were to be patented and held in trust for twenty-five years. After allotments were made, the surplus lands were to be sold and the proceeds deposited to the credit of the Indians in the United States Treasury. It further conferred citizenship on Indians who had established permanent homes on allotments and had adopted what the Treaty called the *habit of civilization.*

"Initially, the Dawes Act was applied only to Fond du Lac, as far as Minnesota reservations were concerned. The act which accelerated allotment proceedings in Minnesota was the so-called Nelson Act of 1889, an act which was designed especially for this state. This act frankly recognized the importance of timber in the area under agreement and provided for an immediate classification of lands into *pine lands* and *agricultural lands* to facilitate settlement of Indians on the one hand, and the sale of timber on the other.

"Although it had once been the intent of Congress . . . to remove all Indians to White Earth, a clause was inserted during the last stages of the hearings on the Nelson bill which permitted those Indians who wished to remain on their original reservations, to remain there undisturbed. This provision, and the 1891 reduction of the size of the allotment from one hundred and sixty to eighty acres seemed, superficially at any rate, to nullify the intent of the bill."

About the same time, in 1889, the "Red Lake group approved the surrender of lands outside defined reservation boundaries. Although the agreement said that the lands were reserved for filling allotments, the Red Lake Band has not yet taken up individual allotments.

"Following the passage of the Nelson Act, another commission was appointed to meet with the Indians and explain the provisions of the new act. This commission experienced some difficulty in persuading Indians to leave their reservations and take up residence at White Earth. . . .

"The state of Minnesota until the present has passed very little legislation dealing with the Indians. The State's constitution, however, does provide . . . that persons of mixed white and Indian blood who have *adopted the customs and habits of civilization* and full bloods who have *adopted the language, customs and habits of civilization* and passed an examination by the district court had the right to vote. . . . It is only fair to note that, on the occasion of the June 1953 Conference on Minnesota Indians, the statement was made by one reservation delegate that, in their county, only Indians who could read and write English were permitted to vote. Since a literacy test is not required by the State Constitution, such a restriction, if true, would be improper.

"One of the most delicate and difficult problems so far as these treaties are concerned is, of course, Indian claims. Another is the problem of the right of Indians to hunt and fish at will on their own reservation, not subject to state regulation. Now, three Minnesota Chippewa treaties—that with the Chippewa of Lake Superior, Fond du Lac, Grand Portage and Bois Fort Bands in 1854, that with the Chippewa Nation in 1837, and the Treaty of 1842 . . . between the United States and the Chippewa of Lake Superior and the Mississippi, that treaty affecting primarily the Wisconsin band, although it did involve a small amount of Minnesota land—claim to guarantee to the Indians the privilege of hunting, fishing and taking wild rice on the lands, rivers and lakes in the ceded territory, during the pleasure of the President of the United States. By statute, Minnesota has declared a policy to discharge in part what is called a moral obligation to the Indians by regulating wild rice harvesting on state public waters, and granting to the Indians the exclusive right to harvest the wild rice crop on all public waters within the original boundaries of White Earth, Leech Lake, Nett Lake, Vermilion, Grand Portage, Fond du Lac, and Mille Lacs Reservations.

"The problem of fish and game is a little different. The state has declared, by statute, that ownership of all wild animals and aquatic vegetation is in the state. Now, this has created a very difficult and perplexing problem of state game wardens enforcing, or trying to enforce, state game laws on Indian land. . . .

"In an 1899 case, an Indian living on the White Earth Reservation killed a number of deer for barter or sale on the reservation. The state sued to get the deer meat. The court ruled that since the state had, in 1899, permitted the tribal government to exist within its borders, it could not do any act to destroy that government. The court said that this tradition of agreement and cooperation between the state and the tribal government had sufficient force to give the tribes the right to hunt and fish within the reservation. The court added that, by its conduct from the time of the treaties on, the United States had assumed and had acted as if the Indians had this right and the state had acted as if it agreed with that assumption."

"In 1930, a case came before the state supreme court where an Indian was taking muskrat out of season. He was a member of the Leech Lake Band and took the muskrat on lands which had been allotted to him but were held in trust by the federal government. The Minnesota Supreme Court held that land held in trust by the United States for an individual Indian, or for a tribe collectively, is Indian country. That Indians living on their allotments or reservations are wards of the United States and thus the state cannot punish an Indian for violations of state game laws committed on reservation or trust allotted lands.

"The last case which I will cite to you briefly occurred in 1944 where a member of the Leech Lake Reservation was convicted of shooting three partridges on land which had been allotted, not to him but to his grandmother, but held in trust by the United States. The supreme court said that it made no difference whether the right to hunt and fish was reserved to a particular tribe in a particular treaty, or not, because the treaties were only grants of rights from the Indians to the federal government and all rights remained in the Indians unless granted away in treaties. On this point, they had the support of a decision of the United States Supreme Court.

"However, this problem is a difficult one and it is being raised in connection with Public Law 280, extending state, civil and criminal jurisdiction to Indians lands. Does this mean that the state can now enforce its game laws on the reservation?

"This question remains unanswered. In the Jackson case, the last one I cited to you from the Minnesota Supreme Court in 1944, the court, almost as an afterthought, suggests that if state laws were to extend in whole or in part to tribal Indians on reservations, it would have to be done by a special act of Congress. . . .

"So the only solution to this problem will come when a case comes before the Minnesota Supreme Court the next time. It seems to me," John Killen concluded, "the court can say that this conception of wardship . . . has to do with the relationship between the Indians and federal government so far as land is concerned and that so long as the United States holds title to the land the concept of wardship prevails and, therefore, the state cannot extend its game laws."

"Have we a right to hunt on the reservation?" asked George Skinaway, who lived at East Lake near McGregor, Minnesota. His question was clear and direct, but in the word wars between the tribes and the federal government there are never clear answers.

"The only ones who can actually make that determination and tell you whether you have an actual right are the courts of Minnesota," responded John Killen, "and perhaps eventually the Supreme Court of the United States. It is very difficult to come to an exact point. . . ."

"I am a delegate," said George Skinaway, "I have to go back and tell the people." He waited for an answer from the white experts. There were no answers to his question. The survivors listened but there were no clear answers.

John Killen discussed several other cases to illustrate the problem of answering questions and finding solutions about treaties. "This is all I have to say to you so far as the treaties are concerned. I know that many of you have ideas and perhaps problems which may indicate a solution far different from the result that I have indicated. Basically, my intention was to raise these problems in connection with the Indians, in connection with the treaties. These are the problems that are going to have to be solved, and as I said, I do not feel that I can solve them. . . . The solution depends upon considering these treaties and also upon considering when not to be bound by them. . . . Perhaps the federal government does not place as much importance on them as the Indians and other people interested in the treaty problems do. These are problems that are going to have to be met and have to be faced before we can achieve a really significant solution."

"My brother is living on our reservation," said George Skinaway. "Now, a game warden came along and took his net." He waited for an answer.

"Which reservation was this?" asked Robert McClure.

"East Lake," answered Skinaway.

"And *your* net was taken?" asked John Killen.

"Yes."

"I think the suggestion that this gentleman here made," said John Killen pointing to a participant at the conference who made reference to Attorney General Miles Lord, "is the better solution: to go to the county attorney to get an opinion from the Attorney General of the state of Minnesota as to exactly how the rights of Indians to hunt and fish are affected."

"Getting back to Public Law 280," said Joe Vizenor, the tribal business manager for the Minnesota Chippewa Tribe from Cass Lake. "When that was presented to our Minnesota Chippewa Tribe, we went on record approving it with the provisions whereby we reserved our rights to fish, hunt, trap, and rice on our reservations. That was written in that law, and it seems to me that should clarify it.

"It should," said Robert Mcclure.

"Well," Vizenor continued, "we have game wardens up there who are pinching Indians right and left for setting nets. We went to our Indian Office and we contacted the United States Attorney and we haven't a decision yet. We should like to know where we're standing, as quick as we can find out."

"This may be a good suggestion," said Robert McClure. "Why don't all of us here who can, in counties which are affected, see if we can't get the county attorney to ask the Attorney General to write an opinion? I'll undertake to talk to the Attorney General myself, to get him ready for writing it, when it comes."

"I don't know whether we can get the county attorneys to stick out their necks that far," said Vizenor. He smiled and nodded his head in agreement with universal political behavior.

"I'm county attorney in Cass County, Minnesota," said Edward Rogers from Walker, Minnesota, "and I have more Indian in my blood than most of the Indians in the state. I am rising in support, or in defense, of the game wardens and the county attorney in northern Minnesota. I can answer these questions which have been asked.

"The first case was the Campbell case on the White Earth Reservation which established the law that Indians belonging to the White Earth Reservation could hunt on that reservation. The second case was the Roy case, on Roy Lake, on the White Earth Reservation. He was trapping muskrat out of season on the lake. The case established this law that any Minnesota Indian who has received a patent-in-fee for his land is by that very act subject to all of the laws of the state, both civil and criminal. I have been trying to educate the Indians in Minnesota about that case. If they have received a payment-in-fee, they become subject to all laws of the state, both civil and criminal same as any white man. That is the law.

"Then, the third case is the Cloud case. It is an Indian trapping muskrat on his own land. He can do that," explained Rogers.

"The fourth case is the Jackson case, which established the law that any tribal Indian could hunt on an allotment. It doesn't have to be his own allotment. It was held that any allotment was the same as a reservation. Now, that is that law. . . .

"But, the confiscation of nets, let me answer that question. Has anybody got any allotment on any lake? All lakes in the state of Minnesota are public waters and you can't take an allotment on any lake. And, lakes are entirely under the jurisdiction of the state of Minnesota and the Game and Fish Department, and if anybody sets a net on these public lakes, they are doing it in violation of law and the net can be confiscated. . . ."

"I would like to make a brief point," said Graham Holmes, Regional Solicitor for the United States Department of the Interor from Aberdeen, South Dakota, "to point out that I have seen this happen in many places: as the population becomes more concentrated, the game is going to disappear. Unless you get together with the state and pass conservation laws together, in a few years you won't have any game at all. It is going to take the concentrated effort and will of all of us, both Indians and non-Indians, if we are to preserve all of our game.

"The reason you have game now, in Indian country, is perhaps because of the game conservation laws. If everybody hunted without interference, we would use up the game and the fish, too, in perhaps a year."

"If you listen to some people, you'd think that only Indians were breaking the laws on hunting," said Joe Vizenor, smiling and nodding once more around the conference room. "In our country, they catch more white men than they do Indians."

"Thank you for your participation," said Robert McClure. "We shall adjourn for luncheon." The participants turned to each other and exchanged personal stories. The conference continued that afternoon.

TRIBAL TRICKSTERS AND SHAMANS

Blue Moon Ceremonial

> The Lumbee also suggest, by lacking what are thought to be "traditional" Indian customs and traits, that Indianness is based in an orientation toward life, a sense of the past, "a state of mind." . . . It is the *way* of doing and being that is "Indian," not what is done or the blood quantum of the doer."
>
> Karen Blu, *The Lumbee Problem*

There we were, eight mixedblood scholars from various tribal times and places, stacked in silence like the mountains around us, shoulder to shoulder on the cold plastic seats in the airport limousine.

More than a hundred tribal scholars, never mind how we were found and selected, had been invited to attend the Convocation of American Indian Scholars. We arrived in Denver; then, with fashionable blond skiers, we flew to Aspen, the first academic intersection between the mountains, where we boarded the limousine for the slow drive to our three-day meeting at the Aspen Institute.

Our silence seemed to be a ritual reversal, time bound, on the secular wake between sentences and terminal degrees.

Listen, we were tribal scholars. Crows, snow on the mountains, and the timberline crossed our eyes. We touched at the shoulders and those too stout, at the hips, but we were strangers, immigrants from the oral tradition on the macadam road to new tribal academe. Some of us must have dreamed our escapes as agents provocateurs, tricksters, and impostors, cautious about the meaning of the word *scholar* and the responsibilities for bearing and wearing strange categorical names from new patrons.

An elected tribal official and a tribal economist, a nonreservation mixedblood, were perched in the front seat beside the driver. In the second row, a medical doctor, a lawyer, and an anthropologist, and in the back row next to me, a college teacher on the left and a graduate public health student on the right.

The elected tribal official turned his head toward the back of the limousine, lowered his sunglasses, smiled, and then returned his gaze to the mountains. We were silent, and then the tribal official called out from the mountains: "Do any of you skin scholars know what a seven-course tribal dinner is?"

From the back the muscles at the base of his neck rolled when he spoke, and his ears seemed to turn forward, cupped toward the primal mountains, more noticeable because his hair was short, black, and erect.

We waited in silence, watched the mountains move under the clouds, and avoided the comment from the elected tribal official in the front seat. The anthropologist whistled once as she exhaled her breath in slow bursts of disgust, perhaps abhorrence.

"Sixpack and a puppy!'

"Shit on a shoe string, too," said the tribal economist perched next to the tribal humorist. He turned his silver head from side to side through the mountains, expressing, as we did in the back rows, a restrained pleasure over our reception of racial insensitivities.

We laughed.

The mountains turned right on time.

We laughed.

We were tribal mummers, strangers on our first shared ride as scholars, and it was crude reservation humor that reduced our distance.

The stories continued in the limousine.

"Applesauce is never red."

"Do you know how to find the medicine man on the White Earth Reservation?" asked the college teacher, a sociologist, as he pinched the loose skin under his chin.

"No, how?"

"Find a blonde nurse with a bottle of castor oil."

"What the Lone Ranger never knew all those years," explained the medical doctor in a slow deliberate speech, "is that when Tonto called him *kimo sabe* it meant *shithead.*"

"Shithead is right."

"This country needs a good *injun* tune up."

"Here we are, brute scholars," said the anthropologist as she shouldered her pouch and leaned toward the door, too eager to escape from the limousine and our forced racist humor.

The mistress of the convocation, with well-placed foundation friends and connections to cash flow, stood masked behind narrow dark glasses, obstructing the mountains in the limousine side window. When she opened the door, a thin smile slid across one side of her face like a crack on a saucer.

"Welcome, scholars," said the mistress of the convocation. "Follow me to the main desk where you will check in and receive your room assignment. . . . No substitutions. . . . Dinner will be at six, be on time, this is not an Indian time conference. . . . We are scholars here."

"Clement Beaulieu," she said as she turned from the desk to welcome me. Her smile cracked on both sides of her thin pale face. "You are in room ten on the end of the building."

I turned down the covers on the bed near the window in the sunlight to rest before dinner. The mountains were personal, but I could not shed thoughts about our first evening session with tribal scholars from reservations and urban centers around the nation. These were the same tribal faces that appeared at all other conferences. Would our visage and language change because we were invited as scholars?

Commercial conversation awakened me. Five people were standing near my bed, looking down at a low table covered with beadwork, including various necklaces, earrings, pouches, and plains chokers.

"What the hell is this?"

"This, well, this is a floral beaded belt," said a stout tribal woman. "Who are you, and what are you doing in bed?"

"Could this be the end of the road for me. . . . hell is a convocation of bush scholars at a beadwork marketplace?"

"Hey pardner, we must be bunkin mates," said a law graduate with a dozen necklaces draped over his forearm. He wore a beaded tie, a beaded belt, two beaded necklaces with thunderbird and turtle designs, geometric beaded cuffs, a beaded billfold, and a choker around his neck made with large black beads, brass, and plastic bones, and he was one scholar to avoid at all costs. He was a law school graduate but failed the state bar examination several times so he turned to the bead trade at tribal conferences. He carried two suitcases, he explained with the flourish of a used-car salesman, one for his clothes, which were stuffed in at random, and the second for his beadwork business, which was neat and well organized.

This mixedblood scholar was a decorated veteran combat pilot. A decade later, the sorties and enemies changed, he combined his failure on the bar examination with beads. He smiled wide over his beads; missing were his two front teeth.

The beadwork marketplace beside the bed and his constant boasting about airborne sorties and law suits bothered me, but when he learned that my luggage was lost between flights, he opened his first suitcase, with no liberal hesitation, and pulled out shorts, socks, and a shirt for me, and then offered to share his toothbrush—a generous and unusual friend and new scholar.

The first convocation dinner, served in the manner of rich families, we thought, at a pleasant rite of passage, was worth the flight in foul weather and a beadwork secular ceremonial in plastic beads.

The mistress of the convocation, who seemed too thin to breathe, lingered on some of her vowels as she introduced the unusual repast and the collection of nervous scholars sitting in several circles like decorated ducks at a feed pond.

Tribal anthropologists and tropical fruits, doctors and lawyers and economists and fresh seafood, teachers and nut breads, elected tribal officials and fowl and rare meats, student scholars and desserts, but no intoxicants, she explained with a more dramatic voice. "There will be no drinking here; we are scholars and alcohol does not contribute to sound mental activities. . . . The hotel bar will be closed while we are here. . . . Eat well and nourish your minds."

Indeed, the bar was closed. The bartender waited in a darkened corner, and with proper hesitation, he asked each patron with light skin for identification. Dark skin was obvious.

New tribal scholars: we were victims in a ritual reversal to the time bind when the tribes were forbidden to purchase or drink intoxicants. The reversal in this case included all mixedbloods who were associated as convocation scholars. To keep us from the bars in town the mistress of the convocation restricted the use of the limousine. We were prisoners in new categories, with new patrons, but we ate well and considered fruit and bread fermentation bowls in our rooms.

Later, when the first convocation meeting had ended, the scholars retreated in the dark to their rooms. The tribal mixedblood economist, who shared space with a medical doctor, invited me and several others, the scholars who were on the limousine, less the bead trader and law graduate, to his room for a drink.

The mistress of the convocation was not successful in her prohibition on drinking. Her instructions were clear, we studied the words hard, but prohibition failed. She ordered the hotel management to disconnect the ice machine, but never disheartened with limitations, we mined a bucket of ice from a sunless vein in the foothills around the hotel.

"Aspen ice abounds," we said, imitating the slow speech sounds of the mistress of prohibition. "Never, never, never, drink a drink without ice. . . ."

"Denial improves the taste, bar or no bar."

"Natural ice is a natural food."

"Toasts to the tricksters."

"Tricksters walk backwards in the dark."

"Ice visions."

"Down the sacred turtle hatch."

"None for me," sounded the medical doctor who was perched on a bench in front of a large mirror. "Indians should never touch alcohol; it kills the brain and poisons our cultures." When he spoke his lips seemed still, motionless, ventriloquial condition, but his eyes bounced like bees from stamen to stamen.

Sitting on the beds, desks, and floor, we examined places in various categories as scholars. We considered the condition of being tribal and a scholar. Caught like animals at a new bait on the old trails with no choice but to devour our minds, as animals chew their flesh free from the traps. Missing parts, invented identities, tribal humiliation, became the remembrance notes in the dominant culture. We decided, less the doctor, that we were our own best memories and that academic accolades were deceptive, word contraries from tribal opposition and inversions.

While we chipped natural ice, drank cheap whiskey and vodka, and told stories in twos and threes around the room, the medical doctor hunkered alone in front of the mirror. He ran his short fingers through his black hair, and from time to time one finger lingered to pick at a small wart on the back of his head, at the hairline. We watched in the mirror, the learned tribal index at the wild treeline, while his face seemed to turn free from his reflection.

A tall and lean warrior moved to his appointed place in the circle and opened the two identical metal suitcases on the counter. He removed his suit coat and white shirt and other clothing which he placed in the suitcase at his left. Then with ritual care he opened the suitcase on his right which contained his feather and beaded vestments, his tribal academicals, and dressed for the sacred dance in the secular hotel room. He wore a breech cloth, a choker with a bear claw on a swatch of leather, a breastplate, a chicken feather bustle, ankle and knee bells, beaded natural tanned moccasins, and in his right hand he held an eagle feather.

The medical doctor scholar disappeared in the mirror, transformed from the warrior tradition of the tribal past, disciplined and alert. He turned with unusual grace, motions in honor of the past, toward the decadence of the present in the hotel room. We waited, natural ice in hand, for the secular reversal, while his solemn gaze toured the room and our faces on the beds. Then the blended woodland and plains warrior invention mounted a record on his small phonograph, lowered the needle, and turned from the mirror. We waited for the harsh war dance music to break the silence, and then the hotel room shuddered from his primal howl. His broad feet pounded the earth, thunderclouds whirled in over the mountains and cracked with the dance in sacred interior space.

"How rapid is the reversion from medical sciences to savagism," said the tribal mixedblood economist as he raised his head, his smile, and his glass to the dancer. "Here we have an example of the loneliness of the ersatz primitive dancer in cultural isolation, whatever would we do without feathers, commercial chicken feathers no less?"

We watched the doctor scholar dance, hunch over, and turn. The plains music demanded our attention, or movement; the dancer controlled our vision, even in stained chicken feathers, and even when we smiled, but did not laugh, at the comments of the economist.

"What sort of a primitive backward savage would dance alone and call that a culture?" The economist combined a sneer with his familiar smile. His silver head turned from side to side as he continued to mock the dancer. "These woodland tribes are so isolated, never a culture, so alone, paranoid from too much wind in the trees; no wonder the fools believe the clouds come to them from their dance; nothing else would come to that music."

The economist, a Lumbee Indian, came from rural Robeson County in North Carolina. Once known as "free persons of color," the Lumbees are a mixedblood people with no treaties, no reservations or tribal languages, who have sought and earned national recognition as a tribal culture. The mixedblood economist is an example of new tribal achievements, comfortable as a scholar in a white padded chair.

The doctor caught the last beat of the dance music with his right foot and stopped, bells silent. His face seemed to slip as he turned to the mirror, the thunderclouds lifted, and his shoulders slumped forward in a familiar posture. The medical doctor, *anishinaabe* mixedblood, who was born on a federal reservation and spoke a tribal language, practiced medicine in a public health hospital but was not at ease in white institutions.

"I dance to disappear in the white world," said the doctor, unlacing the bells at his knees. "You should not laugh at our sacred dance when you have no dance of your own. . . . The dance is not a mouth full of fast words."

The ice cracked in the alcohol. We could hear the economist and the medical doctor breathing, but we were silent.

In her book, *The Lumbee Problem,* Karen Blu writes that there are "two major aspects of Indian identity. One is an articulate, well formulated aspect, which is essentially an explanation, an intellectual account of the origins of the group couched in terms that are meaningful to relevant outsiders. . . . The second is inarticulately expressed and only loosely ill formulated, an often unselfconscious moral and emotional blueprint. . . ."

At the first convocation session there had been a discussion about Lumbee identities. A Commanche from Oklahoma wondered "what criteria, if any, were used by the government in not recognizing your people as Indian tribes?"

"Well, you could get into a definition of culture," responded Adolph Dial, a Lumbee and a historian. "But I know what you are asking. You are saying are Lumbees like Commanches. Right?"

"Yes," said the Commanche.

"And Navajo or some other groups. And I would say that we are quite different. On the other hand, I would like to point out that with all the obstacles, we have been one of the most progressive groups . . . and I am not trying to take anything away from anyone. . . ." said Adolph Dial. He looked around, examined the tribal faces at the convocation.

"The question is, how do you determine whether an individual is a Lumbee?" he continued. "One writer said once that a Lumbee is what he says he is. How do you like that one?"

"I am the words I speak," responded the mixedblood economist, as he moved his silver head from side to side. "We are all mixedbloods, dear doctor, but we are not all aspirants to complete the artifact parts of the past. . . . You bear the absurdities of two pretend worlds in two separate suitcases, and somewhere between worlds you dance in fake feathers in a hotel room. . . . Tell me that a person should be proud of that. . . . proud that we are invented, and so well invented by the white man that we believe we are real."

"These are chicken feathers, for sure," responded the doctor.

His face turned dark red, and his black hair bristled like a porcupine. "But at least I have a dance and I am not from a fake tribe from a fake place."

"More ice," said the anthropologist.

"Fake tribes are alive and well in all of us here," the economist said as he stood near the window. Behind him, the snow on the mountains turned dark blue. He smiled and moved his silver head.

"Dance with your mouth," said the doctor.

"Indeed, a civilized step," said the economist who loosened his expensive tie and shuffled to the end of the hotel room near the doctor. He turned from the mirror and smiled. We smiled back and he laughed, a low sound that seemed to come from far across a dark lake.

"Laughter is no dance," said the doctor.

"You are dead wrong, doctor feathers," said the economist as he turned from the mirror. "Now ladies, and gentlemen, and savages, permit me to demonstrate our traditional tribal dance. . . . First, it is important to emphasize that our sacred dance is not in isolation; we choose to share the mind and the flesh in hand with a woman in our dance.

"Come dance in a sacred time with me," said the economist as he leaned forward and reached for the hand of the graduate student in public health. She hesitated at first, but reassured by his smile and silver hair she moved near him to dance. He placed his right hand on her shoulder and his left hand on her thin waist, and then he turned toward the beds again, where we were sitting, eager to witness his tribal dance. He explained, arms poised on the graduate student, that his people were much more civilized than the "paranoid woodland egotists. . . . Now, savages and others, watch and listen to our sacred tribal dance."

The mixedblood economist whispered in the ear of the graduate student and then he flounced in triple time, a silent waltz. We laughed and laughed, and then he drew his partner close to his cheek and silver hair and undulated across the hotel room floor.

"This is our sacred music," he said, turning around in slow motion in the mirror. His silver hair bounced from side to side, his shoulders seemed to float, and he smiled, the smile that precedes the exposure of secrets and satire, and then he started to sing. His voice was deep, distant, and resonated in the secular hotel room.

He sang the song *Blue Moon.*

"Evil bastard," said the doctor.

"No, Rogers and Hart," said the graduate student.

"Blue moon ceremonials," said the economist.

"Call the spirits back home before dark," said the college teacher. We laughed because it was so serious, he burped, and the tribal anthropologist rolled down between the beds and wagged her feet in the manner of laughter.

Mouse Proof Martin

A word, after all, is a sign for a thing, an action, a quality, or a condition, and signs have a way of breaking loose from their fixed positions or of being uprooted from them. When time, duration, enters in as a protracted influence the word as sign may come to find itself at a great remove from the actuality it was once employed to indicate . . . words live, as we do, in time, and can escape neither its ravages nor its deceptions . . . one intellectural problem is that of bringing such verbal presences and histories into coherence with our own.

Richard Gilman, *Decadence: The Strange Life of an Epithet*

Mouse Proof Martin mounted the round wooden swivel perch in the center of the classroom, removed his mauve beret, smiled, a thin smile that curved like a slice of melon, and then he reached into his leather pouch and tossed various unmatched high-heeled shoes, plastic sandals, worn steel-toed boots, and a few broken slippers with ribbons and bows, to the students seated in a course on race and culture.

"Shoes are common cultural shrines. . . . Examine with care these special single shoes," said the special lecturer to the students as he turned on his perch. "Consider the construction, design, wear and tear, and tell me, as the world turns, about the culture and the people who wore these shoes."

The students, undergraduates with no experience in tribal trickeries, wrinkled their noses over the well-worn shoes and then like terminal dancers the shoes were dropped to the floor and pushed aside, out of sight and smell.

"Shit kickers," said a student.

"Now then, before you expose me as a shoe shaman or a fool with a shoe fetish," said the fool with a shoe fetish as he turned on his perch faster and faster. "Consider the inversion of this experience, the upsidedown insideout shoe show. . . . White people collect moccasins and are forever shoving old tribal shoes under our noses for cultural identification."

The students laughed.

Mouse Proof turned on his perch, started and stopped his motion with no apparent source of power. "Now about words," he said, "words are like moccasins on the trail, old shoes . . . we wear them for different reasons and some seem more comfortable than others, better made with softer leather on the tongue."

The students moaned and hissed.

Moccasin droppers in the white world and name and word droppers from tribal places portion out their sham in the same conversations from time to time. Beaded moccasins, preserved or worn thin, are dropped with curious admiration, a marvel to civilization, while the tribal name dropper turns his words with mythic resonance.

Mouse Proof is about as subtle as a conventional mouse trap, but he is a memorable tribal name dropper, including his own, which he dropped more often than his shoes. His name, he explained to the students, is much more than a bad translation. He was eleven, short and smart with one slack ear, a mixedblood orphan and survivor from an unnamed coastal tribe, when white words first encroached on the animals and birds and ancestors in his dreams and visions. The orphan was an experienced fisherman and spoke three tribal languages when he was forced to attend a federal boarding school on the reservation, where, on his knees and elbows beneath an organ, he learned to read and write *mouse proof,* his first two colonial words. Mouse Proof waited at the fair feet of his teacher when she played the organ in the classroom. There on the two foot peddles which were pumped to fill the bellows, the two words of his name-to-come were printed in steel. He was attached to his teacher, her feet and ankles, and the words under her feet. He turned beneath the organ and looked up her dress into the darkness of her crotch as she perched on the edge of the stool, while he traced with his fingers the shapes of the letters in *mouse proof* until he could read and write the words with pure passion. The first word to come was *proof,* slow and smooth into the oral traditions of his memories, and then the word *mouse* burst in his vision like an enormous fur animal. He wrote these words on all the reservation walls and desks, on walks, boards, and intersections, water cans, and birch trunks; scratched the words on stone, and with love for his teacher, he tattooed *mouse proof* on the ten fingers of his small fists. Federal school administrators accused him of *tribal turpitude,* but the students cheered his accomplishments, his passions for a white widow woman and two white words, and held farcical nickname ceremonies at the foot of the organ, where *mouse proof* became his tribal name.

Later, much later, he learned the words *trap* and *shit,* but his cultural transformation beneath the organ, from an oral to a written consciousness, troubled him because he had lost the reasons for being near the feet of his teacher. She must have sensed his unnatural need to grovel beneath the organ at her feet and so she redirected his energies. She took the first two words, *mouse* and *proof,* the third and fourth words, *trap* and *shit,* and in six months with variations on these four words, she added three thousand more to his cultural transformation. Mouse Proof turned his visual stimulation from her feet to her lips, as she pronounced thousands of words for him, and to her fingers, as she wrote words on the blackboard. Her white flesh was no darker than the chalk.

Mouse Proof turned on his perch from side to side, face to face, with an unnatural power. He told the students that he would tell stories about tribal transformation, atavistic and holistic migration, and moccasin shaman flight, but first the mixedblood trickster introduced six *tekosid,* or little people, from tilted dreams, uprooted trees, uneven worlds, and memories from his own seams and dreams which he failed to mention in his introduction.

"The little people fill these old shoes with words," said Mouse Proof Martin. "Shrines to our lost comedies."

SIX TEKOSID LITTLE PEOPLE

Erdupps MacChurbbs, a senior woodland sprite who travels on words in all directions and in all memories through tribal time.

Sophia Libertina, the dark woodland lover of the little trickster, and others she will not name, who dresses in leather and white linen and wears fingerbells, and filoplumes on her ears and thin ankles.

Bishop Friedrich Baraga, the old-world latinist, a short man with tall missions, who wears a verdant green dalmatic and weeps over swaddling clothes.

Rachel Hill Boeckmann, daughter of James Jerome Hill, the famous railroader, who lived with her surgeon husband, and later, when she returned as a little person out of time to her mansion, she lived with her memories, retired celibate church officials, the new owner of her mansion, his roomers, women, and two cats.

Vane Territorial, the metatribal diatribist who smokes too much and raves through slow histories at the bottom lines.

Girlie Blahswomann, a tribal mixedblood former promqueen and feminine ideologist, who has turned to road maps because she lost her place in the world.

Mouse Proof turned on his perch and said that the little people would appear like faces from dreams in four scenes. He smiled and told his stories as he turned.

BIRDS ARE NOT HUMAN

Erdupps MacChurbbs, the mythic woodland *tekosid* sprite, snapped like a spark through uncommon time and space in the warm morning sun from a half-cocked indoor lemon tree bough to a winter coleus in a mustard pot.

"Migration takes place in the mind," said the little compassionate master of tribal trickeries. He was standing at the rim of the pot beneath canopies of red leaves in the Rachel Hill Boeckmann mansion on Summit Avenue in Saint Paul, an erect and perpendicular place. "Migration is a natural tilt, through time and cracked windows."

"Not migration," exclaimed Sophia Libertina, the little woodland lover to the little trickster, "but immigration. . . . tell about immigrants from other times and places." Sophia was dressed in leather and white linen and black filoplumes suspended from here ears. She danced across the dining room table sounding her fingerbells.

"Sit down here under the coleus and listen," said MacChurbbs, spreading his fingers over his face like a mask. The little trickster possessed the imaginative power to change his shape in visions and memories. He conducted himself in the dreams of others, larger than he is known at home. From time to time his hands and feet and ears and other parts are different sizes. For a face mask he imagines his hand larger. He dreams his hand larger, the power of imagination. "Listen now, migration is spiritual immigration and immigration is political migration under hand, humor is freedom, chaos divine, and tilted dreams are the best worlds in which to dream."

"But, but we are more than migrating birds."

"But, but, butts are spun from the faces of static fools. . . . Birds, much to their credit, are not human," said the trickster, smiling through his fingers, "but, but, but humans, much to their credit, are birds."

"Consciousness. . . ."

"Consciousness imagined and won," he said.

"Won what?"

"Migration memories," he said.

"Nor are words our real dream states of being," said the woodland sprite. He snapped his fingers four times and then snapped like a winter spark from beneath the coleus to a pendant on the chandelier in the drawing room. "The tribes migrate on their voices from creation while dominant culture domestics tick tock through time-measured ideologies from place to place in eventless advertisements."

"Words are words are words. . . ."

"The oral tradition is not a written word," said the woodland trickster. "Written words immigrate, the tribal voice migrates in visions from the creation. . . . We are earthdivers in our dreams, not mere word mongers."

"No wonder we are called earthmothers."

"White men wash their hands and remember nothing."

"Soap remembers them."

HOLISTIC IMMIGRATION

"Vane Territorial, the metatribal advocate, floats through words, telling in cathedral tones his holistic concepts of cultural movements and immigration from post to post and pendant," explained the trickster as he swung with his linen-dressed lover from the faceted pendant. "He will be here soon. . . . The smell of words precedes him."

Sunbeams burst from their word perch in the chandelier into heart-shaped rainbows across the ceiling, flashed over the carved wooden eagle above the fireplace, and spread over the rumps of three sheep in a painting on the east wall of the mansion.

"You must mean holistic migration."

"When territories are unmoved, measured, and spaced, the earth and her divers become institutions," said MacChurbbs to Libertina, shivering on the pendant and shivering the rainbows around the room. "Vane Territorial is a migrant historian, from and content tumble through his electronic memories like memoranda in an institution. His essential material, linear word dreams, and timebound stories connect little more than lexical sounds. Territorial is a tree trunk in an oral traditional wind, imaginative leaves rattle above him, but he remembers little more than bound words. He is not a bird, he is a post on a prairie."

The rainbows dipped and wagged.

Mouse Proof smiled as he turned on his perch.

Sophia Libertina sounded her fingerbells over the lecture tones of the trickster. "Little man, you are so boring," she said, leaping from facet to facet, pendant to pendant. "You could become all the words you speak. . . . Imagine that tangled word vine somewhere in the universe."

MacChurbbs continued: "His imagination and past memories colonize the space where he stands, the artist captures movement in written words, the final blows of the word shaman. . . . People from the oral tradition dreamed out from the wilderness, bear immigrants at the treelines of civilization, new *worders*, holistic written word migrants, tricking their listeners and immigration biographers into the past over their stories."

"You are some mouth warrior,' said Libertina, dancing in space and sounding her fingerbells. "One enormous mouth warrior." The sound of her bells filled the mansion. The cats came up from the basement to listen and to watch the little people on the chandelier and on the fireplace mantels.

Rainbows swooped beneath the eagle and over the cats.

Mouse Proof turned backward on his perch, around and around backward, until he seemed dazed from motion. But nothing stopped his stories or his words. Compared to the characters in his stories he was, without a doubt, the little diatribist, Vane Territorial.

RAILROAD MIGRANTS

The compassionate trickster pumped and pumped the pendant faster and faster until the rainbows turned the room around like the spirits from a tribal sand painting.

"Earthdivers change the earth," said MacChurbbs.

"You are a holistic migrant fool to drag our tribal past through the cedar smoke into this cold old mansion," said Libertina with her hands resting on her narrow hips. "Men are nothing but *worddivers,* not *earthdivers.*" She smiled and snapped from view. The cats blinked and licked their paws beneath the sheep. The rainbows wavered.

When the rainbows turned slower the trickster snapped from view, following his lover out of time and place. The pendant stopped, the house was silent. Wordless in memories. Places motionless with no voices. Painted sheep stopped in faded paint on the hills.

Time started and stopped.

The cats waited on the windowsills.

Rachel Hill Boeckmann, daughter of James Jerome Hill, the famous railroader, built the mansion where the woodland sprites and benign demons snapped through time from room to room, dream to dream, word to place and backward.

Bishop Friedrich Baraga, the old-world linguist and mission sprite, bearing a small sprig of white pine from an eagle nest, and dressed in a verdant green dalmatic and black satin hat with a ragged tassle, was kneeling on the narrow mantel over the marble fireplace in the dining room, stroking his white beard.

Beneath him the familiar railroaders dropped their verbs and sipped their wine in word-wound events out of time. Bishop Baraga frowned; his brows rose and folded in latinized boredom over his troubled gaze. Baraga published the first lexicon of *anishinaabemowin,* entitled *A Dictionary of the Otchipwe Language.* He entered the tribal word *tekosid* for a small person or little people. Little did he know then that he would become a real *tekosid* woodland sprite.

"Where is MacChurbbs?" asked Baraga.

"He is listening to a humanist priest and watching the fit dowager of this old mansion thump her cane and purse her lips in the drawing room," said Libertina, as she blinked twice and turned in space like a windblown catkin.

"Rachel Hill Boeckmann?"

"Rachel Hill Boeckmann, the railroad and medical widow and dowager is with James Shannon, President of Saint Thomas College, the one who speaks so well in humor with his hands and brows," said Libertina. "His gestures bear the best rituals from the tribal past."

"The metaphor here is old mission time," said the little woodland bishop, as he lifted from the mantel and soared through the room. "Listen to this unusual migration out of time."

Rachel Hill Boeckmann thumped and thumped her cane between her narrow shoes. The sound bounced from room to room like an echo in a flume and then escaped through a fireplace flue. Shannon spread his most generous smile between his bulbous cheeks and drew his good breath between historical railroad litanies. His voice migrated on ideals over the prairie and through the mountains, over the rails from coast to coast and letter to letter. The old dowager thumped and thumped her cane to his magical tune. Shannon tipped his head to the right, his benediction gesture;

the dowager smiled and confessed that she would spare the private papers of her father, his letters and memorabilia for future migrants to ride the barren rails into the unsettled but protected past.

"Time wears her metamasks with grace," chanted Baraga as he soared through the mansion, his dalmatic folded on sacred slipstreams between the pendants on the chandelier.

Mouse Proof blinked four times and smiled.

FASTFOOD SCENARIOS

"Tribal earthdivers migrated as spirits, windblown mountain flowers, birds and animals, when their words were creation myths in the oral tradition," said MacChurbbs to Baraga. The trickster was back riding the sheep through the painting on the east wall of the mansion.

"The settlers from the old world escaped nothing, moving in fear of the unknown over water and woodland," explained Baraga, "but the civilized places in their heads, our heads, and the church in our hearts, never changed. We changed places but not our minds." Baraga rode with the trickster on the sheep through the painting.

"The escapees denied science, tribal shamans, resisted the theories of blood circulation, the revolutions of the earth, motion, and tacit migration," snapped the trickster from the painting. "The old-world escapees forever burn on their terminal templates, abstract maps, religious scenarios, burn the last bridges from the wilderness, the unconscious, from their civilized heads, and leave their shadows behind to flounder forever in political ideologies."

"The shadowless have no mind to migrate," said the trickster from the rump of a sheep. "The shadowless move in constant fastfood scenarios from familiar place to place in place of dreams. The shadowless followed the earthdivers into the dark woodland, cut the tress, lost their earth souls, and ended their adventurous lives eating fastfood in isolation."

Mouse Proof twirled on his perch.

BANAL RETENTION

The *tekosid* bishop soared closer to the pendants on the chandelier in the drawing room. In his sacred slipstream the facets rolled rainbow waves over the trickster sprite on his sheep.

"Remember the map woman?" asked MacChurbbs.

"Good old Girlie Blahswomann," said Libertina who snapped back from her distant dreams. Blahsmann was a South Dakota-born tribal mixedblood promqueen turned Kundalini yogi who squeezed fresh fruit juice near Sather Gate at the University of California in Berkeley. Responding to the demands of radical feminine ideologies, she changed her name from Blahsmann to Blahswomann, lost her center, and disappeared at place names on road maps.

"She suffers from banal retention," said the trickster from his passive sheep. "Losing her rituals, her prairie forms, her migration mind to abstracts and ideologies, she became the old world in eventless words. She even wrote words on her hands like maps to find herself during the day in familiar time and place."

Girlie, growing like a word pile from the tongues of street culture evangelists, tacked a colorprint map to the ceiling of her fruit wagon. Without visual memories from the oral tradition she locates time and place and her reservation families and friends on maps. Her linear thoughts move in written words over printed medium territories from the prairie to the desert. . . . She has lost her migration mind. She became what she wrote, a place without shadows in a time without dreams, borrowing personal names and places from ideologies. Her dreams were shadowless, no more personal than advertisements.

The little woodland bishop blessed himself thrice and then wheeled down the facets on the pendants. The rainbows bounded and his face turned red and white and then his brows folded over like caterpillars.

"Girlie is domesticated like some animals and all political escapees from the old word world," said the trickster riding though the rainbows out of breath. "Domestics never migrate out of time. . . ."

Rainbows bounced again over sheep.

Mouse Proof cleared his throat and turned backward.

The trickster bounced out of time. "Domestic animals lose their animalness, caged birds their birdness, tribal people on federal reservations their tribalness. . . . Domestics are escapees with no minds to migrate from the cold elevators and mimics caught in cultural word wars," said Erdupps MacChurbbs.

"Down with elevators," said Libertina, sounding her fingerbells. The rainbows stopped. The mansion was silent. The *tekosid* little people from the woodland snapped back to tilted dreams and half-cocked migration centers in the mind. The cats returned to the basement.

Mouse Proof turned on his perch and smiled.

The students threw back the shoes.

Mouse Proof examined each shoe and identified the tribe, the place, woodland, desert, plains, urban concrete, while the students shuffled to the exit doors.

Bells rang and the hour changed.

Natural Tilts

The abandoned earth, overtaxed with words, choking in knowledge, and with no living ear on it to listen into the cold. . . . It would be nice to take each man apart into his animals and then come to a thorough and soothing agreement with them.

Elias Canetti, *The Human Province*

Erdupps MacChurbbs, the shaman sprite from the tribal world of woodland dreams and visions, shinnied up a sumac shrub and tiptoed out on a branch to watch the sun rise one more time over the river. Standing at his side, in the tall cool weeds, Mouse Proof Martin talked with the tribal trickster about the weather, the sun, the death of the river in the cities, and then he turned the discussion to half-cocked appearances of *tekosid,* or little people, in worlds with natural tilts.

Mouse Proof Martin told him that he seemed much taller, much less foolish, than the last time the two had met. MacChurbbs, smiled and winked over his right shoulder.

"Erdupps MacChurbbs, would you tell a few stories for the readers here about little people and tribal trickeries, and perhaps a word or two on the triumphs and tragedies in tilted worlds?" His tone was serious.

Silence.

The sun burst through the sumac leaves.

"What has become of the tribe and little people in the cities?" Mouse Proof asked in a more casual tone of voice.

Silence.

"Will our families survive pollution?"

Silence.

Mosquitoes buzzed around his ankles.

"Poison rains?"

Silence.

"Will the river survive?'

Silence.

Erdupps MacChurbbs, the compassionate tribal trickster, shinnied out on the highest branch above his head. There, behind a row of red leaves, in the first flash of sunlight, he snapped his fingers four times, pinched his small lips, and became a river otter. He was transformed in the sumac, much larger than he was as a little person. The branch broke with the change, a sharp snap that sounded down the river near the limits between the cities, and the trickster otter dropped through the leaves and slid down the riverbank chattering and clucking in his varied voices. He seemed pleased as he bounced down through the weeds.

Some shaman sprites and tricksters are spiritual healers, with warm hands and small medicine bundles loaded with secret remedies, and some shaman spirits are clowns who can tell and reveal the opposites of the world in sacred reversals, natural tilts in double visions, interior glories. The shaman clowns and tricksters are transformed in familiar places and spaces from common grammars, the past and the present, in the shape of animals and birds.

"MacChurbbs, where are you?"

"Smallpox and the river are dead," chattered the trickster otter from the river shore below. The first flash of sunlight glanced over the dark water, turned and burned on the trash, cans and cartons, plastics, and shimmered over a rainbow of oil film from paint poured into the river.

Silence.

MacChurbbs, the river otter, winked, clapped his paws like a clown, and then flapped up the riverbank transformed as a common black crow.

"People have lost their connections to the earth," said the crow in magical flight from the river. "People have forgotten when to surrender to imagination, and when to dive into the earth face and fact first. . . . In tribal dreams the little people, tricksters and clowns, are the earthdivers from all times and places."

Shaman crow preened in the sun on her perch in the sumac. Her dark eyes, and the red leaves, flashed in the new sun. "Once upon a time, we were all leaves, like these leaves around us and the leaves floating in the river. Once we showed our teeth under water in myths. . . . but now, the foolish giants have become machines more than leaves, and we are no longer important to our myths," she crowed.

"The river is dead, lost to pollution and eventless words, not because the river was evil, but because the white man and his machines are evil, because the white man is separated from the sacred connections to the earth. . . . The white man has lost his face to machines, turned from the earth to seek mechanical immortalities. . . . Smallpox and the river and myths are dead."

"Listen," said Mouse Proof, chewing on a strand of sweet weed, "there are white and tribal fools at all the intersections, at all the dumping places in all the rivers; myths may be nothing more than social repression. . . . So what is this wild white man mask for the sins of industries?"

Shaman crow listened to Mouse Proof with her head cocked too far to the right. The sun glanced on her tilted beak, shivered on her feathers, and threw her shadow on the tall wet weeds on the bank above the sumac.

Silence.

While Mouse Proof was looking down, brushing the mosquitoes from his ankles, he heard the peaceful sound of bells. When he looked up the crow had disappeared and there on a sumac bough was a little person hidden under a plain brown bag.

"Who are you?"

"Erdupps MacChurbbs," she said, disguising her voice as best she could. She winked and smiled under the bag.

"Sure, the ultimate dream," said Mouse Proof.

"The fantastic woman in the man becomes his own lover."

"Be real."

"One black crow," she crowed.

"Who are you?"

"Sophia Libertina," she said in a gentle voice, "here alone to liberate your fears and free your secret dreams." She sounded her finger bells.

"Free me then. . . . be quick about it."

"Once upon a time, we were the river," she said once more in a different voice from the sumac. "Now, the river flows through the cities, but not through the people. The river is dead, leaves are down with no teeth. The mean white man is separated, cured from his smallpox disease, but cursed with machines. . . . The place to dive back into the earth is lost.

"The white man waits alone in the poison rain on the riverbank with his fishing pole. The child in the white man died between the dead river and his dead machines, surrounded with bouquets of plastic flowers. The river shivers, the plastic cracks in the cold."

Silence.

"Cultures that poison rivers are cultures of sorcerers," shaman crow continued. "The sorcerers must be outwitted, not defeated like evil, but outwitted, to resurrect the river and the sacred connections between the tilted earth and our dreams."

The sun burst through spider webs.

"Even blind men find their way," said Mouse Proof.

Mosquitoes bit him out of reach.

"Listen to the plastic crack, crack, crack."

Sophia Libertina danced backward on the bough as a crow to tell stories about an old mixedblood shaman who found an urban connection, a place to dive back into the tilted earth, a way back to the sacred through landfill meditation.

"Martin Bear Charme," she said as she sounded her finger bells and whirled on the bough in the sun, "founder of the Landfill Meditation Reservation, was undereducated for urban survival, but he put his unusual mind to the earth and made a fortune hauling trash and filling wetlands with solid waste and urban swill. . . . The status of a trash hauler is one of the best measures of how separated a culture is from the earth, from the the smell of its own waste.

"Bear Charme teaches that we should turn our minds back to the earth, the rich smell of the tilted earth. We are the garbage, he told me once in magical flight as a crow. We are the *real* waste and cannot separate ourselves like machines, clean and dumped, trashed out back in the river. We are the earthdivers and dreamers, and the holistic waste. . . . We cannot be detached and perfect between the refuse and the refusers without losing our place on the earth. The earth and the river never forget where we dump our waste."

"Charme chanted *come to the landfill and focus on real waste,"* shaman crow crowed backward on her perch in the sumac. *"Mandala mulch, and transcend the grammatical word rivers, clean talk, and terminal creeds,* and put the mind back to earth. Dive back to the earth, *come backward to meditate on trash* and swill and *real* waste that binds us to our bodies and the earth.

"Charme made millions in landfill, enough to hire his own lawyer, a madman thrashed in trash, who petitioned the federal government for recognition as a sovereign tax-free meditation reservation, a place where laws and liens are intuitive. . . . shamanic flight should be recognized as a duty-free port," crowed shaman crow as she winked and ruffled her black neck feathers.

"Where is the landfiller now?" asked Mouse Proof.

"Bear Charme is still soaring duty-free through the mind trash out west near the ocean," crowed shaman crow and then she preened backward in silence. The sun burst in small rainbows on her feathers. She turned and then thrust her black beak through the red leaves, in the tribal manner, toward a person who was walking down the riverbank.

Melvin McCosh, the gentle and elusive bookseller from a refined retirement home in the suburbs, was driving down the river road with his enormous white dog at his side. He was driving to an estate sale to examine a collection of art books when he saw Mouse Proof stranded deep in wet weeds.

"Mouse Proof was talking to a crow with the voice of a little woman in a sumac shrub," he explained in several stories later. McCosh stopped to reassure Mouse Proof that the state of the world, and the state of his mind, were much more troubled than he had ever imagined in conversations with little people.

"Melvin McCosh, please meet Sophia Libertina," said Mouse Proof, pointing over his shoulder. But when he turned the bough was bare and the *tekosid* leather and linen princess in a crow had disappeared.

McCosh stroked his white beard and, not without his own realities, he told stories about his animals, white dog and two other mixedblood mongrels. "These dumb dogs love books. . . . They sleep on them, eat some of them, follow the scent of a good title from room to room," he said, looking up the riverbank to his book van and the white dog posing as the driver, "but not one of those dumb dogs ever learned how to read a single word."

"Listen McCosh, she was dancing right here on this bough," said Mouse Proof, ignoring his universal animal stories.

"Neither can we."

"Who said that?"

"The animals," said the voice from somewhere in the sumac shrub. "The little animals from the woodland. . . . Dogs read more than grammars."

When McCosh raised his left hand to stroke his beard, his watch slid down his thin wrist and dropped into the weeds and hit a beer can. The sound distracted his attention to the material loss, and when he turned back to the sumac a stout woodland *tekosid* sprite was perched in a small crotch of the shrub.

"So, it was your voice."

"The animals speak and read through me," said Vane Territorial, the *tekosid* metatribal diatribist. The little sprite corners and breaks his words like a bronco buster.

"Now, back to talk about the river?"

"The river is a language," said Vane Territorial as he lit a small cigar. "The word course that floods the lowland fools . . . we all take from the river, claim space with words, and then turn silent in time."

"Language is as dead as the river."

"Language is never dead."

"The river is our industrial hope chest," said McCosh, who seemed to linger over the curls of smoke from the little cigar. He smiled and then saluted a barge passing on the river. The barge was filled with road salt for the winter.

"But the river is dead."

"Language and the river look like death because words and

water bear the dead dreams from your time," said Vane Territorial. The wind moved his hair but nothing more. Smoke seemed to move about him in the shapes of animals as he spoke. The diatribist was not animated; his words were broken from interior road maps and material visions.

"Neither is the wind," he said.

"What?" they asked and waited.

"The wind is not dead, but like language and the river, it bears the poisons of the time," he explained between curls of smoke.

Silence.

The sun broke above the sumac and threw out tilted shadows into the weeds, and the bridge dropped over the rail into the water.

Mosquitoes circled their ankles.

White dog barked from the book van.

McCosh laced his fingers into the shape of a massive spider web over his white beard and bowed to the woodland sprites in the sumac. Then he smiled and climbed the riverbank back to his van and continued his drive to an estate sale.

Vane Territorial disappeared in his own smoke. The bridge wavered and the crows crowed down the tilted river.

Paraday Chicken Pluck

So the poor man suffers doubly. No longer boosted by the women on the one hand, and actually competed with by them on the other, he feels depotentiated and unable to rise to the heights expected of him. All this at the same time as he is rightfully developing his own more sensitive feminine side.

Irene Claremont de Castillejo, *Knowing Woman*

Mixedblood women are no more accountable for the craziness and lunancies of tribal men than are the beaver to blame for diversions in headdress and troubles in the fur trade.

"Still and all," said Happie Comes Last Screamer with her head cocked to the right, "we do get blamed and blamed and blamed." Her fancies are avian motions, common chickens in a pinch or pluck, rather than fur bearers.

Happie bears no blame for the beaver or the fantasies of fur traders. Her troubles are over dark tribal men. The unrest started like the fur trade, solemn totemic ceremonies to honor those animals with broad flat tails, sensuous influences under birch wood, semiaquatic fur scores with new traders, cocked felt hats, competition on the trap lines, economic imbalance, and the strange behavior of tribal men. Her troubles started and stopped with new fashions overseas.

Happie Comes Last Screamer came back from overseas, and she is sure to mention *overseas* several times, even though she lived on an island in a lake, which is her manner to invite discussion on her travels with tribal men. She returned to the mission boarding school, where she lived as an orphan, divorced her husband, Amik Screamer, and then she relocated in the west near a *real* ocean. Happie dropped her married name, altered her interior dreams, and tried to lose the memories of reservation tribal men and the past she once remembered as sacred.

Amik Screamer, a dream name and nickname given to him when he was seventeen and in love with an older white woman who taught school on the reservation, was a fanciful tribal dancer, a serious drinker, and, in recent time, a blanket and canvas squatter with his fair mixedblood woman on a dark wooded intersection near a sliver of the Bad River Reservation on Madeline Island, one of the Apostle Islands in Lake Superior.

His dream name is related to an unusual experience. When he was thirteen, while he waited in a duck blind at dawn he fell asleep and dreamed that seven enormous beaver were screaming at him from all directions. He screamed back, a deep primal scream that scared the ducks, even the elders on the hunt. A shaman, who was asked to give meaning to the dream, said that the "screamers were white rats from the cities. . . ." The shaman named him *gichi waawaabigonoojii,* which means *big mouse,* but the beaver image prevailed. Amik, which means *beaver* in the language of the woodland *anishinaabeg,* a tongue he learned in the oral tradition, danced in the sun, the moon, in the rain, under thunderbirds, dreams, and sacred visions, over wind, water; he danced as he breathed, more than he walked or even worked, and he drank as much as he danced, beer and wine over all the stars in the universe. The spirits from the dance, the consuming spirits from the tribal past, and the shivers when he drank too much too often, separated him from the mixedblood woman who loved him with few reservations.

"These brush hammers dance for nothing, a few bucks prize, a drink; their feet move in simpleminded pride," complained Happie Comes Last Screamer while she was still overseas. "But not much footwork or sex for their wives. . . . That damn fool would sooner dance for the weather than a woman. . . . He can take the rain to bed without me now."

Amik Screamer never trusted traders; he set no snares or traps for beaver. He danced and drank into the past. He mentioned but one trap in his experience, that "pale-skinned woman waiting at home with her arms out. . . . She spreads her arms like a tree waiting for me to fall in."

Happie Comes Last held out her arms for months and months in the dark. She endured the present, the dull spaces between his dance dreams into the past, between the slow tumbles in his traditional voices, fetid breath from cheap wine, and his hostile attention to tribal women with darker skin, until she discovered that he masturbated over pornographic pictures on a high red rock overlooking the lake.

Happie followed him one morning through a thunderstorm, through the dark trees and lightning because she was suspicious that he was on his way to meet a woman. There were women on the rock with him, in retouched color, but not in the flesh. She watched at a distance while he climbed to his prurient cache in the crotch of a white pine tree, and then over pornographic pictures of white and black women, an inflated plastic blonde, which he inflated next to him, and several pairs of firm foam breasts formed from famous female movie actors, he mounted the high red rock.

Happie watched him seek his sexual pleasures alone and then she came back from overseas. She cried and cried for several months and confessed to the sisters at the mission school and then she took her tribal name and moved west.

"Pictures and plastic more than me," explained Happie Comes Last.

"The world is a strange place," allowed the sisters.

"Stranger still with a dance," she responded, "he never loved no one but a picture. . . . He can dance on those pictures and forget me."

Happie turned into the thunderclouds and rode the hard shoulders of personal histories and measured chances over the mountains and down to the ocean. There, in the watercities now, she labors full-time in a simple healthfood cooperative, where she sorts dried organic fruits, rotates the produce, cuts imported cheeses, and learns the intrigues and conspiracies in a new tribal world. She also studies meditation and writes stories from a tribal perspective for the *Mountain Meditator,* a critical tabloid on meditation and holistic health and healing.

"The fur trade is still the fur trade."

Happie Comes Last has a weekend horse in the hills. Three times a week she mounts a colorprint of her stable old stallion on the cash register before she tallies the sales. When the customers admire her mount she tosses her hair back, light brown near her mouth, and cuts her eyes to the right and blinks several times.

Happie lives in perfect time now, Mother Superior tells the nuns back home on the reservation, but even pure and free mineral water and all the organic food she can eat do not build immunities to the same old tribal ups and downs of real row living. Twice each month, on the down time, she drops in at the *Paraday Chicken Pluck* on Telegraph Avenue and Haste Street and plucks the stiff tail feathers and lesser sickles from the rumps of more than a dozen common white roosters. Plucking chickens, she whispers to herself, balances an imperfect world.

Catholic Convent
Lost Nation Mission School

Dear Mother Superior:

I bought a new pair of boots last week, soft and stiff at the same time. The lemon sugar cookies from the sisters were delicious, but you know how we all feel about sugar out here.

Sweet William is not feeling well this week. His back shivers and he favors his left side, so we walked and talked the trails over the weekend, until he felt better and took me on for a short ride home. He is a gentle mount, and he moves with grace.

Nor have I been feeling well all the time. There is a muscle virus going around, but it is a different sort of down feeling than having a virus. I have it worked out now, I think. No, it is not a man again; the problem has been resolved with chickens, not men, this time.

Yes, chickens, plain farm fowl, but let me explain the problem first. In the past year I have awakened several mornings when there did not seem to be a measure for time, when I felt too much alone, days that did not connect from past to present, and did not seem to exist, dates that I could not think about much, much less remember as real time. Time that has no time, no calendars, time when time does not exist in time. Well, rather than spend my time in some sad *abusement* park avoiding the feeling, I went to check it out with my astrologer friend and psychic reader, especially after these days were coming up two or three times a month, or more. Well, I was told by both of them that Jupiter, the fifth planet from the sun, was passing near the earth—how have you been feeling? They insisted that I find a place to spend sanscalendar time plucking feathers from chickens. Such craziness, plucking chickens? Somewhere on a farm they thought because I came from a farm, well, really, the mission farm there?

Well, as I have often told you, you can find anything you want out here in the watercities, except water, maybe. San Francisco is beautiful, especially during a sunset, but I like living in Orinda, over the hills, just in case the big earthquake comes.

Paraday Chicken Pluck is the name of the place where I go when I wake up on one of those *nontimes*. Plucking is a kind of torture, like running out to the henhouse to abuse the chickens, that puts me in touch with my feelings again. Strange, but better than abusing myself, the people at the cooperative, or Sweet William.

Justice Pardone Cozener, interesting name huh, the short fat sweet mixedblood man who conducts the *Paraday Chicken Pluck*, is just wonderful to me. He is a failed lawyer and teacher, and it makes him mellow to pluck. Failure is so good for the spirit. Last week he gave me three extra chickens to pluck in a private room. He calls the whole operation the "good times away from time. . . . everyday is a paraday for someone." He is the first man who has paid attention to me without lust on his mind.

We can both go plucking when you come out to visit next month. Remember to bring along the extra brown paper bags. Stay away from sugar. Cancer is in everything.

Happie Comes Last is Happie Happie.

Justice Pardone Cozener was convicted on three counts of gross imposition to brown pullets and a white rooster in the South Dakota Swine and Chicken Court and sentenced to labor six months on the state chicken ranch for domestic fowl offenders or to leave the state and not return for ten years.

Justice Pardone, who claims tribal blood from an unknown tribe, was working as a tribal lawyer on the reservation when he took a liking to chickens at certain times when he could not recognize time. He accepted banishment and moved back to the edge in the watercities.

Ten years earlier, he had launched his corrupt career as a teacher of various metaphysical themes at a reservation college with no walls, no degrees, and no credits. He became one of the federal feedlot bigbellies of the tribes and did himself in on fastport and herbs and roadman dreams from too much dope before his lectures. The students called him the result of a "common urban vision." His no-credit courses were not renewed.

Unable to find work as a teacher and having failed the bar exam three times, he settled on a reservation federal feedlot legal program until he imposed himself on the sacred state bird.

With the cash settlements from lawsuits against several universities for discrimination, Feedlot Cozener opened the first chicken-plucking center in the world. He still operates the original *Paraday Chicken Pluck* center, and in two years has sold nine grants and charters for similar centers in seven states.

Chicken plucking was a cover, at first, for cocking mains in the basement, but the public needed to pluck pullets did so well upstairs that cockfighting is now scheduled only when the champion Shawlnecks, Baltimore Topknots, White Piles, Irish Grays, or White Earth Half Breeds are in town. Then the bigbellies massage their cocking birds to erect warriors and thrust them at each other in the basement.

Feedlot Cozener is supplied with imperfect chickens from several state chicken hatcheries and farms. From one capon hatcher he gets myopic cockerels. The castrated birds run around with their heads down chasing the little people.

Erdupps MacChurbbs, the woodland sprite and compassionate trickster, and Sophia Libertina, the little dark woman dressed in leather and linen, were poised on the upper rack of the pillories in the center of the center where the public plucking is conducted. For three dollars an hour one can pluck enough feathers to make a hat or a fake tribal headdress. Behind the two sprites and the public chicken pillories were five booths for private plucking.

Libertina sounded her fingerbells and tiptoed down the pillories over the rows of nervous white pullets while MacChurbbs snapped through time and space from booth to booth observing the private plucking. The booths were named for five varieties of domestic chickens.

Cornish Plucking Booth

"Touch me mother. . . . Pluck the hackles first and then the saddles and touch me in the pits. . . . Touch me in the pits and sits," said a plucker in the private booth.

"Then we will roll you on the summer spit," said the compassionate trickster who was riding on the points of a fat red comb.

"Who said that, mother?"

Plymouth Rock Plucking Booth

"With these feathers plucked down from wicked sickles and sinful butts. . . . The spirit is with me and thee counting these feathers plucked from shame and sin. . . . The spirit is with me and thee counting these feathers plucked from shame and sin. . . . Now our inner chickens are free from evil and sin," said a plucker in the second booth.

"The spirit is a domestic bird," said the woodland sprite.

"The spirit is a bird," said the plucker, a white nun.

"The spirit is a plucked chicken chicken chicken," said the trickster and then snapped from the comb in one booth to the fat brown hens, in the next plucking world.

New Hampshire Plucking Booth

"Up your tight droppers little brown pullets," said a plucker in the third booth. "For fifteen years that rotten evil woman of mine forced me to clean up your shit while she protected your asses from the good ax, but now she is gone, gone for good, buried in chicken shit up to her neck back on the farm. . . . Now you miserable birds are going down feather by feather, and these old farm hands are going to squeeze the last drop of white rotting shit out of you for good."

"Deliver me oohhhh great farm woman from this world of chicken shit dreams," said the sprite, snapping wattle to comb on the brown hens.

"Who said that?"

"The monarch of chicken shit," said the sprite.

"Goddamn talking shit," said the farmer as he grabbed three chickens by the short legs with his massive hands and bounced them up and down on the floor until white chicken shit covered his wrists. The farmer ground his false teeth together from side to side and sounded three bleats like a sheep.

Dorking Plucking Booth

"Where will the chickens in your old word garden grow?" asked Erdupps MacChurbbs as he hopped through the hackles. Libertina sounded her fingerbells to a pace quicker than his casual movements. The plucker in the fourth booth looked up from his feather count, over his librarian lenses, and smiled. His teeth were stained. "You little ones have blessed me with your return," he said, blushing, and wagged his long eyebrows. "You have returned to hear the count. . . . Garden indeed, there is something for us all in a chicken feather, and so we count and count and sort the colors from the perfect patterns of the natural world found under our chickens."

"You are a fool without feathers. . . . Stupid time out of time counting feathers stupid stupid stupid," said the compassionate trickster.

"Not stupid," the plucker insisted, as he lighted a cigar, "chickens are my game in the field of feathers. Feathers have a logic of their own."

"Fowl fields," said Libertina.

"These feathers on the oldest breeds of domestic fowl," said the counter, "are my fields." Foul smelling smoke from his cigar filled the small plucking booth. Libertina pinched her nose.

"More than the chickens know?"

"No doubt about that," he responded with a hard smile, "have you little people ever seen a chicken counting his own feathers?"

"Chickens are not stupid," said MacChurbbs, snapping from the hackles on the first chicken to the wattle on the second.

"But you are stupid because you have invented a field of useless information, categorical comparisons of the comparisons that have been compared, what reason would a chicken have for a feather pattern count?"

"Then we are all stupid."

"Stupid information is made for stupid people, people who are mistaken in the watercities," said the compassionate trickster.

"But this booth, mister little perfect, these chickens, and their feathers once a week are all the fields I will ever know in the distance between our worlds, our lives, and urban consciousness," said the plucker. He resumed his feather count. Libertina snapped through space to his outer ear and whispered that she loved him in words and feathers.

Rhode Island Red Plucking Booth

"In the last private plucking booth, a small white woman with white hair and a compulsive need to rebuild the world with little shrines, her shoes, tickets to the racetrack, her travels and visions, all sounds and gestures placed in the world as shrines, was singing to three plump hens. The chickens clucked back cluck cluck cluck.

"She sounds more like a chicken than a person does," said the compassionate trickster, holding his hands in the shape of a sacred shrine. "Could you, little white woman, be part pullet?"

"There is a chicken inside all of us," she said, "one full feathered fowl inside is worth three in the bush, and the park *derangers* are all camped out tonight cluck cluck cluck. . . . Do you know how to hold hands in a shrine, little one?"

Libertina snapped through time and space to the feather saddle of the middle hen. There she removed her small red shoes, lifted her linen dress to the waist, and slid down the feathers through the sickles to the main tail.

"Are you certain?"

"This plucking place puts me back in place with our inner chickens. . . . You see, too many *derangers* want to pluck our inner chickens for what is said to be for our own good. . . . Teachers, salespeople, all take a pluck at our inner chicken when they have a chance, until the inner hens and roosters are naked, ashamed, and unable to flop in flight. . . . This is a good place to pluck back our inner chickens. We are all related to the wild red jungle fowl inside; how else could we have survived all the pecking and plucking throughout our lives."

"Are you certain?'

"Certain is certain about the mean inner pluckers. Protect the inner and the outer cocks and pullets from mean psychiatrists and social workers and fast talking healers."

"Does your inner chicken ever crap?"

"Ceremonial."

"Ceremonial crap?"

"Ceremonial chicken shit," she said, cocking her head to the right, and then she continued cluck cluck clucking to her outer and inner chickens. Libertina sounded her fingerbells three times, and then the two little people snapped from view, snapped from the chicken plucking center, snapped out of their minds, snapped through time and space from the watercities and the lost worlds of plucked inner chickens back to the whole time and place of dreams and wild flowers in domestic fields.

Happie Comes Last plucked back from her inner chicken from overseas and clucked time back together until it was dark. Her world comes together on the pluck.

Rubie Blue Welcome

> The activities of the trickster figure often show the first of a series of operations for turning the common-sense, everyday lifeworld into nonsense. . . . The systematic violation of categories and norms of behavior that the trickster presents appears as a negation, a reversal, an inversion, of those cultural categories and behavior norms that make up common sense. . . . As the embodiment of disparate domains, trickster is analogous to the process of metaphor, the incorporation of opposites into a new configuration.
>
> Susan Stewart, *Nonsense*

What the new tribal world needs is a better puppet to balance the tense distances between reservations and cities, a satirical puppet to modulate the differences between men and women, mixedbloods and others. Not the human varieties of puppets who are invented and manipulated in the white world, but the hand-animated characters with real hollow heads.

The following imaginative confession comes from a tribal graduate student who once served as an informer for several covert intelligence agencies. Cedarbird is his name, his personal and his code name, and he wrote this in his secret notes and later in a satirical novel.

Rubie Blue Welcome is separated from the sacred with names and numbers, but she has a puppet with whom she celebrates her distance from tribal men and mother earth. She took up her first name from the color of her lips and turned to academe in place of dreams, linear theories over intuition, visions, and personal experiences. Rubie is ruled with words, grammatical inventions, not a sacred *blue welcome,* not the color on a woodland lake high in the mountains, but a secular translation and animated word pile beside a swimming pool.

Rubie Blue Welcome is better at words than most mixedblood skins, and she has a puppet to advance her derision of tribal men, which is a special disadvantage for us because we would never satirize tribal women with a female puppet. We choose shaman puppets and little people to express and explain our dominance and power in the world.

Some names, like some puppets, have power. The power in a name, in a word, is determined by the source of the word, and how or when the name is dreamed and first spoken.

The official name on my birth certificate, for example, is the name I will not reveal to strangers. I am a mixedblood from the plains, born normal, which is a claim most puppets make, under a whole moon in a public health hospital. The official name has become my secret name, a secular reversal, while I am known by the descriptive name *cedarbird* which I assumed in school.

Some tribal names are given as nicknames, some are borrowed and dreamed, and some are stolen, but descriptive names in translation are too far from sacred to hold power. Traditional skins, or tribal people, seldom revealed their secrets or told their sacred dream names to white missionaries for translation. Now, we live in new worlds and new words, assuming animal and bird names to be different from white people, which is superficial and political, not a vision, and to suit the tribal image as a public invention.

When some of us mixedblood skins took on bird and animal names in middle school on the reservation, two generations after nicknames and tribal sacred names were forbidden, the white teachers made us write all three names—the first, the descriptive, and the last name—a hundred times. Those teachers must have thought that tribal names were diseases. In college when we were expected to be walking and talking puppets from the traditional tribal past, we dropped our first and last names and became known in the white academic world by our descriptive names. We pretended that these names were sacred names in translation.

So, here we are now, translated and invented skins, separated and severed like dandelions from the sacred and caught alive in words in the cities. We are aliens in our own traditions; the white man has settled with his estranged words right in the middle of our sacred past.

Severed from sacred places where we once lived without measured time, when we became birds in the morning and turned back from white feeders at dusk, when we became leaves down in a hard summer rain and showed our teeth, and then, we dreamed so much about the past that we became our own invented past. Our time here in the cities is not to confess our invented tribal past in church basements, but our vision is to imagine like earthdivers a new world. We will become what we imagine. N. Scott Momaday said something like that at the Convocation of American Indian Scholars: "We are what we imagine. Our very existence consists in our imagination of ourselves. . . . The greatest tragedy that can befall us is to go unimagined. . . ." We have become unimagined mere first and last names, puppets, the content of our own denials. We have so much to imagine and so little to confess.

My descriptive name is an invention, not a translation, but my secular reversal from the sacred is no different than the separation of Rubie Blue Welcome. We all turn to books and machines, new politics and noise, when we move from reservations to the cities. Words relocated from sacred places became the shape of our visions, not the source of our dreams. We became word and mouth warriors, shadowless memories in the cities. No mountains or rivers or birds without words, no water sounds or wind without weather reports. The common tribal metaphors we once shared stand now in abstract places, statues, eventless in descriptive words. My name is not an event, her name is not an event from dreams. We are translated, invented, and transformed now in plain grammars, not in visions as animals and birds.

In the cities we are forced to be imaginative without spirit.

Some take up the tribal invention to survive, but not me, never. For me, separated from the sacred, but skeptical about tribal fundamentalism, terminal creeds, and political spiritualism, personal power lurks in secrets and trickeries. Secrets become my mythic connections to dreams; trickeries my balance between absurdities.

But enough on tribal philosophies, and urban compensations; these are stories about Rubie Blue Welcome and Four Skin, her hand puppet.

Rubie Blue Welcome is part linguist, part feminist, and an expert on the word piles and lexical loot from the Sun Dance, which was the subject of her thesis. She was the first uninvited speaker at a student protest for control of the department of tribal studies.

Unaware that she was participating in her own demise as a lecturer, she lifted the microphone to her enormous mouth with one hand—her right hand was hidden beneath a small red and blue blanket—pinched her thick brow down on the spring sun at noon, and, in front of the administration building, she said this:

"Let it never be forgotten, students and friends, that there is the sure hand of a woman directing the movements of this dumb little feathered head."

Blue Welcome boomed, hissed, and whistled; her words bounced over the concrete, brick, ceramic tile in the brackish fountain pond. Her speech shivered through the immature leaves on the fists of the pruned sugar maples as she raised the red and blue blanket, presenting a male hand puppet with a tribal headdress made from sparrow feathers.

"Four Skin is his sacred name," explained Blue Welcome. Wriggling her fingers in his stout head, she introduced her modified Tsimshian ceremonial puppet with leather bound arms and oversized plastic hands. She smiled, mouth opened wide, and he blinked his brown plastic lids.

"To me, Four Skin is the minimal tribal man, the man with no woman in him but these three fingers. . . . See how his little mouth moves, how cute, crowing with bad grammar, just like a man." When she pulled her fingers out, his head went limp and dropped forward, reversing the drape of his headdress.

"This little fellow speaks for the last of the noble savages, inventions from the white man, not the woman but the *man,*" she emphasized, thrusting her hand back into his head. "We are in the new world now, where tribal women rule."

Four skins hissed from the audience.

"No woman would have invented a male feathered fool to mimic as a hunter, but the white man did. . . . The hunted, perhaps, but *not* the hunter." She seemed to chant her words about men, raising the whistle in her voice.

Five skins hissed from the audience.

"Women did not cant their medicine secrets and shoot and trap animals for stupid felt hats. . . . Tribal women are the sacred bears and the vision birds now; we gather berries with our hands, not bad dreams about animals. We touch what we eat and return the seeds to the earth; bad dreams about animals turn the water sour."

Six skins hissed from the audience.

Silence.

Seven skins hissed from the audience.

Last month at a linguistics conference when Rubie Blue Welcome burst into another piercing word show, her third attempted prelude to a paper she wrote on tribal feminism, a radical revision showing that tribal men dance over mother earth for father sun and sex, the audience clouded over, thundered, and rained her foreword down.

"Four Skin, Four Skin," the conference skins called and then insisted that she tell about her fine feathered friend. Humiliated once more before dominant tribal men, but never one to turn from a live microphone, she shifted her chin from side to side like a sheep at the fence waiting to be sheared, pulled her puppet out from her shoulder pouch, thrust her hand into his slack head, and then, fingered into animation, she touched her slim nose to his, which seemed to transform her mood from depression to hostilities, and confessed that her puppet was her best friend even though she "hated tribal men who dance all over mother earth for father sun."

The audience, her peers, tribal students, and college teachers, whistled, moaned, and laughed at her performance with the puppet. Most of us then were too serious to snicker and roar in our own satire. There were no white visitors in the room, but for a moment or two at the most, we sacrificed our invented appearances at the conference, rather our ceremonial contraception, for imaginative and sardonic humor.

Blue Welcome, like her puppet, is her own moveable satire, her own race and vanishing text, but she is *no* trickster—we all agreed to that much last quarter in her seminar on tribal languages—because she cannot tell the differences between mythic connections, bad ideas, and theoretical separations.

Four Skin, she confessed, and she is forever confessing something, was her most permanent relationship. Speaking through her puppet, she explained in tedious lecture tones how she has been attached and separated too often, like bad glue, from parents, teachers, and men. "More and more men," she moaned, and then she stuck to women, moved to machines and appliances in time, and then back to women. Now she celebrates her human connections with a puppet. Nothing sacred, nothing lost in material magic.

"Besides," she added, cheek to cheek with Four Skin, "puppets travel with no trouble and are better listeners. . . . But to tell the truth, I might never have finished graduate school without my little Four Skin at my side. Psychiatrists recommend them, mine has two, one for each hand, and she uses them to speak through at therapy sessions." Rubie Blue Welcome smiled, hugged, and kissed her puppet on the forehead, nose, and chin.

"Four Skin," she whispered into the microphone, moving his chin to fit the shape of her speech, "tell all those protesters out there what ever happened to General George Armstrong Custer at the Little Bighorn River?"

"General Custer caught it."

"Caught what?"

"General Custer caught clap from a shepherd," said the puppet in a deep voice. "He got it from a mule who got it from a mule skinner who got it from a sheep who got it from a shepherd who got it from his mother. . . ."

"Never mind."

"Lost that too."

"But tell about his death."

Four Skin presented several tribal and nontribal traditions and inventions: he wore blue circles on his cheeks, beaded buffalo heads on clam shells, plastic bear claws, rabbit bones on a breast plate, breechcloth with a beaded codpiece attached, to emphasize his plastic penile parts, and knee-high moccasins.

"Tell these fine people under the maples how did the white warrior lose his balls?" Blue Welcome shifted her weight from one foot to the other in front of the microphone. Her angular hips seemed to fold at the waist like a giant puppet. She wore high-heeled white shoes, open at the toes. When she moved, the arch on the shoes curved and twisted and the heel tipped, forcing her bulbous brown toes to reach out and touch the concrete like snails. Her right toe rubbed on the rough surface while she conversed with Four Skin.

"Sure."

"How, then?"

"Fine."

"Watch your tongue."

"The mule skinner said that too."

"Never.'

"Sure he did," Four Skin insisted, with his brown plastic chin extended, "General Custer lost the war at the Little Bighorn because he lost his balls the night before. The poor man died not knowing where to find them."

"Is that the truth?"

"Sure is the truth. General Custer lost his balls the night before the battle, but he has returned you know, resurrected now as all women with blonde hair."

"So, that explains it," said Blue Welcome.

"Explains what?"

"Explains the attraction male skins have for blonde women," explained Blue Welcome. She was certain the skins would like that line, but her attempts at humor were received with silence.

"What could be more pleasant and political at the same time?" asked Four Skin, turning his head from side to side and nodding to the audience. "A night with a blonde woman or a night with General Custer?"

Silence.

"Neither," said a person from the audience.

"Who then?" asked Four Skin.

"Buffalo Bill."

"William F. Cody is still a blond."

"Blond wig."

"Illusions are important."

Remember in the movie *Buffalo Bill and the Indians, or Sitting Bull's History Lesson,* by Robert Altman, when Sitting Bull arrives at the circus and Buffalo Bill, played by Paul Newman, does not recognize him because he is too short. Instead he thinks that the tall one, Halsey, played by the Indian actor Will Sampson, is Sitting Bull. How could a famous chief be so short?

"Sitting Bull has said that he is here by the will of the Great Spirits," said Halsey, translating for Sitting Bull, "and by their will he is chief.

"His heart is red and sweet, for whatever he passes near tries to touch him with its tongue, and the bears taste the honey and the green leaves lick the sky. If the Great Spirits have chosen anyone to be leader of their land, know that it is Sitting Bull."

"Halsey," said Buffalo Bill, "you tell the chief Buffalo Bill says his green leaves can turn wherever they want. . . . just so long as they know which way the wind's blowing."

Buffalo Bill ran his hand through his blond hair and then turned toward his show soldiers and said the following out of the side of his mouth: "I think I gave 'em the same murky logic they use on us."

"Sitting Bull says that history is nothing more than disrespect for the dead," responded Halsey, from the other end of the circus tent.

"Blonds on white horses have all the fun," said Four Skin.

"Say good-bye to all the blonds," said Rubie Blue Welcome as the puppet tipped his head to the audience.

"So long Buffalo Bill and General Custer, so long for now."

Rubie Blue Welcome withdrew her hand from the puppet.

Sorrie and the Park Fountain

> I found Rolling Thunder an excellent companion for a walk or a ride or hauling water or pitching a tent or having a simple meal. . . . I have never seen in him the slightest hint of anguish or despair. . . . I am convinced that every image, every moon and every reaction he displays has a purpose. Each day it was becoming clearer to me that Rolling Thunder was a teacher who could offer me insights that I could never achieve in the laboratory or discover in the library.
>
> Doug Boyd, *Rolling Thunder*

Doctor Peter Fountain, the evertribal natural invention and professional dissimilation in the new urban world, called a press conference at a fastfood restaurant to announce that he was a serious candidate for the San Francisco Park Commission.

"To sleep in a park is to love a park," he said. "Parks are sacred places where people come to restore their connections with the earth, and a few women now and then."

Fountain lectured about the need for park reform to fastfood strangers in the burger row, and a few of his tribal friends, but his announcement was lost when the french frier siren sounded a new batch on the line. No *real* loss, but his thick pride was hurt because no reporters answered his telephone calls.

Fountain, the undaunted desert reservation mixedblood, bundled a dozen thirteen-page curriculum vitae under his tattooed arm and delivered his park reform sleeper speech in person to newspaper and television reporters at their offices. Most reporters, centered and conservative over time, disliked being cornered in their own space.

"Mister Watertight, remember me?" he said to an editorial writer for the *San Francisco Chronicle.* "Real name is Doctor Peter Fountain, but friends call me *doc,* plain lowercase *doc,* because there are so few of us with dark skin."

"Well, Mister Fountain, friends *never* call me *watertight,* even in lowercase. . . . Where did you hear that name?"

"From the receptionist," said doc, spreading his thick lips and stout arms to apologize in good humor. "No offense intended, sir . . . when asked for a nickname she offered *watertight.* Seemed in line to me."

"Spare the flack and methane."

"None intended," said doc as he slid unannounced and uninvited into a sculptured wooden chair with a private college seal on the seat and handed the editorial writer a curriculum vitae.

"Park Commission?"

"God rest her good soul," said doc, dropping his smile," poor old woman was robbed and raped behind the rhododendron in her favorite park."

"Who?"

"Marion Frances, the dead park commissioner whose seat I seek in the election a month from now," doc said, elaborating his intention.

"The name was Francis Marion, *he* not *she,*" snapped the editor. "You seem to have trouble with names . . . nicknames for certain."

"Was he not a homosexual then?"

"Who are you?"

"Call me doc, lowercase, the first tribal park commissioner. Let me tell you about the spirit of parks and what we have in mind," said doc with a wide smile to catch and balance a frown on the face of the editor.

"Ten minutes."

"More than fair. . . . Tribal people do more than recreation in parks, we live there," said doc in rapid speech until the editor calmed him down with his hands, "we sleep there, and commune with mother earth in the parks." Doc turned with a wide smile on his face. No one could be more pleased with his own words. "Parks are more like sex than monuments . . . attitudes, use and abuse, give sex and parks meaning and pleasure."

"Golden Gate is a mistress to the tribes, no doubt."

"Tribal people came from reservations to the cities and live in the parks, we are natural outdoor people, and parks are the best hotels in town for us. . . . Remember that we *are* the parks, parks *are* the tribes, because mother earth planned for us both to sleep together."

"Mother earth is a one night stand."

"More than one night, my friend; we love and protect the parks, ask the park police. . . . We live there and civilize the wilderness and the darkness, we make parks livable places for white people who still fear the wilderness in their soul. . . ."

"Two silver stars, bronze star, purple hearts, distinguished citations," said the editorial writer, reading from the curriculum vitae.

"We are tribal immigrants, the new settlers in urban parks," said doc in a low tone, his serious lecture voice. "In the parks we are like white settlers on tribal land, but the difference is that parks are the urban reservations and we are not cutting down the timber and turning the flow of rivers."

"Combat hero, no less."

"Korea."

"What unit?"

"Seventh Cavalry."

"And a scholar, too?"

"Doctorate in clinical psychology from the University of Southern California," said Doctor Peter Fountain, pushing his massive hands down the arms of the wooden chair.

"Yes, I read that here," said the editorial writer, finding his realities in the written word, assertions, and counterclaims, then, as a last resort, in the presence of a person. "Your first college degree was in *nursing?*"

"Yes, served in the medical corps."

"Unusual. . . . Outstanding. . . . Sure do, we can pass the word that you are a serious, and peculiar, candidate for the park commission," said the writer. Looking up, through his rimless glasses, he added: "You know, I was overseas too, I was a combat writer for the newspaper *Stars and Stripes.*"

"The tribes are doubly blessed to have your kind understanding," said doc, sliding out of the sculptured wooden chair. He looked back at the seal on the seat.

"Better doubly blessed than double-crossed, doc. . . . Remember what happened when we signed treaties with *you* people," said the writer. His smile was strained. He opened his palms and shrugged his shoulders. Historical apologies dropped in silence like dead leaves. Then he checked the time on his watch, lighted a cigarette, and walked toward the door. "You and your people are to be admired, doc; best of luck to you in the parks. . . . Sleep well as a commissioner."

When the writer shook hands with doc at the office door, in full view of his receptionist, he held on to admire his unusual tattoos and his vest. Fountain had mountain lions snarling on the back of his hands and knuckles. On each forearm were four beautiful wild flower tattoos. When the tall dark receptionist came over to touch and admire his flowers, doc unbuttoned his fish scaled and rabbit bone vest, revealing his narrow hairless chest. There, tattooed on his chest, a sunset with a row of cottonwood trees, several crows perched, and monument mesas in the background. The mesa landscape scene gave doc the appearance of having a massive chest.

"I am better prepared than anyone to be the new park commissioner," said doc, scratching the trunk of a cottonwood on his chest. The crows moved to the side. "You might say that I have been preparing for this election for a long time. . . . Remember, time is a circle to the tribes, and my vision and sacred name came from the park. . . . I am the park, the park is in me, and in my dreams. The park is more than *harmless abusement.*"

"Divine scene," said the receptionist. "A real landscape with no billboards or power transmission towers. Such a novel idea, the whole wilderness on one chest."

"Interesting observation," said the editorial writer. "I am

impressed by the fact that doc has no words or messages on his flesh, no slogans for mother or the nation."

"We came from the earth, mother earth, and we speak her secret languages in our oral traditions," said doc, buttoning his vest. Darkness returned to the mesas and the cottonwoods. Peter Fountain waited at a bus stop in his interior darkness.

"Oral traditions must be exciting," said the receptionist.

"Come to the park and listen to the tribes at night talk with mother earth; come to the parks, we will be there, and you can watch my sun set," said doc as he waved with one hand, in the invented tribal manner, and turned to leave the editorial suite.

Doc Fountain lives with a short woman who has enormous pure white breasts. Sorrie Permission is her name. She works for the San Francisco Trash Commission and reports that she is a mixedblood from a woodland tribe, or as her white friends tell on her, a *wooden tribe*. Sorrie met the doc one morning last summer in the park where he was sleeping and where she was evaluating the overnight trash. She poked him with her trash prod, and when he rolled over she saw the sunset on his chest through his vest. Time stopped in the park; trash unturned. The next morning doc awakened in her bed, and the two have been living together since then, with occasional overnights in the park.

Permission encouraged the doc to seek a public office, a place on the San Francisco Park Commission. "Who knows more about parks than you do?" she asked. Sorrie also arranged for doc to be a high-paid consultant to the San Francisco Trash Commission. No one, not to mention a tribal person, has ever been paid as a consultant to sleep in the park.

Permission and the doc became the talk of the town—her breasts, trash, park consciousness, and his tribal face and chest—but *their* talk, private and public, was about building the perfect park for the old park tribal sleepers.

"Together, as park skins, we can find the political power to build the perfect park," said Permission. She unfurled their schedules and plans for park power, while she recited several original lines from her poem about the old park sleepers:

the old park sleepers
seek their rest
with restless lovers and quiet feeders
cadent shufflers
brave men from the wilderness
soles patched with matchbook tops
seldom tears
memories of old sleepers
old war cannons in the park
unarmed
tribal histories
turn green and white
underpigeon wings
the world rolls over in sleeping minds
under collars
doors click shut
heroes cast in summer bronze
gather in the park to rest
all the wounded world
moves on worn cobblestones

Doc Fountain is a verbal sailor on a spurious sea, tacking his pretensions to the color of the listeners. Speaking to a conference of urban tribal welfare workers, doc demanded their blood vote for him as park commissioner and told them that the earth in the tribal man, which was corrected by a tribal feminist, has more significance than the color in the person. "Earthdivers dive in all colors," he said.

"Not him again," said a tribal social worker.

"Last month he was still talking about education and reservation economic development," said another social worker, "but no one was listening, so he has changed the subject, and still no one listens."

Doc read from a prepared speech.

The means and measures in the personal portraits of our survival on tribal reservations are tied to white imagination and government support; some white men have earned eagle feathers from the private gardens in our traditional past while some of our own people have lost the trail to progress and wear plastic flowers and chicken feathers. Our pride, my white friends, is your pride; our feathers come from the same birds.

"Brilliant metaphorist."

"You can always tell a smart redskin," said a banker in a dark suit, "because he is the one the other tribesmen will avoid, his ideas are too advanced for the primitives to understand."

"Sounds reasonable for a park commissioner."

"Find the park in your hearts," said doc Fountain at his second press conference, held under the sycamore trees in front of the art museum in Golden Gate Park. There, standing with his lover Sorrie Permission, he announced what his first decision would be when elected a park commissioner. One television station and reporters from two newspapers were there, poised to record a significant historical event.

Doc Fountain unbuttoned his fish scale and rabbit bone vest and exposed the sunset over the mesas on his hairless brown mixedblood chest. "Ladies and gentlemen," said doc with his arms extended and his face turned upward toward the gulls perched on the pruned fists of the sycamore trees, "did the tribes die in treaties with the trees?"

In the cities we have become what we resisted in the past, a sublime invention, wild and clean, primitive and simple, but some of us hang our heads like defeated warriors, shriveled sunflowers, and drunken fools, prime bucks lurking at the treeline in the parks . . . natural ecologists, invoking mother earth in litigation from the chips discarded by the wood carvers on the porch.

The parks in my administration will be places of visions, places where men can come to dream, where men can turn to magic, where men can dowse and burn their pipes in magical flight with medicine men from the old west.

Gulls shifted from fist to fist.

People frowned but listened.

The television cameraman turned toward a reporter and asked for directions between words. "Where is this asshole coming from?"

"Tribal dream parks."

"Now ladies and gentlemen," said doc as he wiped his brow and then continued reading his speech:

The animals trailed and birds flew with us for a time, and our tribal madness made us perfect victims for a perfect culture in the cities. We are needed in the parks now, not as tribal inventions or victims in the white world, stoic on billboard horseback, feathered in white parades, beaded in the suburbs, but we are needed now as deans of the dreams in the parks. Those who spurn these tribal inventions become invisible in the park, imperfect victims.

Gulls shifted on the sycamore fists.

Doc lowered his arms and looked down and around him like a circus master. "Now, in the center circle, ladies and gentlemen, it gives me great pleasure to introduce a great man, a tribal spiritualist, Doc Cloud Burst, the prairie founder and leader of the San Francisco Sun Dancers, who should have a few words about me as the new park commissioner.

"Earth mothers want doctor sons," said a reporter.

"How much does a commissioner get paid?"

"Thirty thousand a year," said a television sound woman. "No wonder he woke up in the park."

"Listen to me now," said Doc Cloud Burst after he stood in silence for several minutes under the sycamore trees. Hundreds of people were in the park and stopped to listen to the tribal speakers. The audience whispered and moved closer to the speaker, like a gentle whirlpool, more interested in the visuals than the verbals. Cloud Burst wore a breastplate, choker, beaded buffalo belt, a black hat, and carried a walking stick and a blanket over his right shoulder.

"Listen, the spirit is with us in the park; we make this park a good place in our visions. . . . The San Francisco Sun Dancers seek their visions on the streets and return to mother nature in the parks," he said, pausing to take up a hand drum which he sounded while he spoke.

"I tell you these things because our brother the doc is the best man to be park commissioner. He has a vision and the earth talks in him about parks. Listen, you can hear the sacred mother park talk through him. . . . He spoke to the four directions on the streets, lived outdoors four nights with no money or food. Not in hotel lobbies or fastfood lines. And then, like all disciples of the San Francisco Sun Dancers, he walked across the Golden Gate Bridge to the ceremonial bunker at Fort Cronkite near Rodeo Lagoon. . . . There, at dawn, he was pierced and received his sacred name which must never be revealed, but I can tell you and the gulls that his sacred name has something to do with the parks, and we knew he would become the first sacred park commissioner. I have stopped talking now."

Several stories about the unusual tribal candidate for the park commission were broadcast on television and published in newspapers. The attention brought doc support from numerous individuals and organizations. His name, and phrases from his speeches, were passed from conversation to conversation like scenes from a new movie.

Political observers were certain that doc could have been elected park commissioner, but too much attention to his past, and his lover on the San Francisco Trash Commission, aroused envious critics. His degrees and achievements listed in his curriculum vitae were published, but doc was not challenged until he appeared on a late-night radio talk show. The host of the show, in preparation for his tribal guest, called around the country to gather more information about Doctor Peter Fountain. The host discovered that no one with that name had received a doctorate in clinical psychology from the University of Southern California. Further, the host discovered that doc was not a decorated hero; rather, he received a medical discharge for mental aberrations. The trap was set for radio; doc was at the studio on time.

"Doc Fountain, welcome, and welcome to our listeners. . . . I have with me for your live questions tonight a person who has become famous overnight," said the radio host on the air. "Two weeks ago he was asleep in the park, and now, now he *could* become the new park commissioner. That person is none other than Doctor Peter Fountain, who answers to the name doc. . . .

"As usual," said the radio host, "we begin each talk show program with a special quotation pertinent to the person being interviewed, and then to the questions. The quote tonight comes from *Ethnopsychoanalysis,* a strange book by George Devereux, who wrote this:

"Ethnic identity is sometimes maximally implemented by those who, by ordinary standards, would not be expected to possess it. . . . Behavior instancing ethnic identity tends to be more ritualistic and monotonous than behavior triggered by the ethnic personality."

"Now doc, how do you explain the fact that two weeks ago you were unknown to the public?" the host asked, tilting his head to listen to the answer.

"Tribal people are invisible in a white world."

"I have a copy of your curriculum vitae which lists, I assume, most of your achievements and professional experiences, and on the first page you tell that you were born in Indian Territory—where is that located?"

"Oklahoma, like the musical."

"Wonderful," said the host. "now folks, in a few minutes, you can start calling in and asking doc some questions, but first let me introduce the *real* man with some questions of my own.

"First, you claim that you graduated from the Chilocco Indian School in Oklahoma, is that right?"

"Yes."

"Are you sure?"

"As sure as a dreamer can be."

"Then how come no one there knows about you?" the host asked, leaning back from the table in the radio studio. He leaned back like a man who had hooked a sunfish.

"Tribal people are invisible in the white world."

"Perhaps you were never there?"

"Chilocco is a bad dream," said doc, unbuttoning his vest and exposing the sunset on his chest. "I can remember it like a picture on the back of my hand . . . let me tell you about the golf course there. . . ."

"Golf course, come on. . . ."

"Right on brother, a golf course is what it was, miniature, of course, located near the water tower," said doc, flashing his mountain lion knuckles.

"Enough miniature golf," said the host, interrupting the game. "I also checked on your military record and educational records, and no one ever heard of a person with your name," said the host, leaning forward for the catch. "Did you ever use a different name?"

"This man has invited me here to abuse the name of tribal people," said doc, buttoning his fish scale vest, dropping his smile, and changing his tone. "You are not the first racist bastard who has abused the tribes, you will not be the last perhaps, but you will not accuse me and get away with it. . . . You are a racist word freak, and you have talked me right out of here. I want nothing to do with you, but at another time, ladies and gentlemen, I will talk with each and all of you again. . . . Come to the park."

"Listen, doc, is it not true, answer this before you leave, is it not true that you, posing as a clinical psychologist, treated people? Are you afraid to answer the question?

"The only thing we found which seems to be the truth is that you are an Indian," said the host, "but Sorrie Permission failed the mixedblood claim; she is from a pure white family that never saw an Indian in three generations. . . . What do you say to that?"

During the week reporters investigated his credentials and discovered that nothing in his curriculum vitae could be verified. The Bureau of Indian Affairs recognized his name but could not locate his reservation or the school he attended. Doc responded to all investigators that "the tribes are invisible in a white world."

Sorrie is white and pretends to be a tribal mixedblood, Peter Fountain is a tribal mixedblood and pretends to be white. Dancers desire the power of poets, politicians dream about wisdom, one sex wants to be another; the world must be realized through inversions and opposites, sacred and secular reversals. Permission once altered her birth certificate to appear more tribal.

Two days before the election for park commissioner, a newspaper published the following editorial column about the spurious candidate with unusual park visions:

Peter Fountain may not be a certified clinical psychologist, but as a park dreamer and tribal leader he is a trusted man with good humor.

In numerous public appearances and on his application as a candidate for the San Francisco Park Commission, Fountain has been identified as a doctor, implying that he has earned the highest academic degree in clinical psychology. A recent investigation of his academic records indicates that the institutions he has listed have no knowledge of his attendance.

In an interview last week, Fountain said he became known as a doctor because of the needs of white people. "They found it easier to talk and work with me as a human being by making me a doctor," said Fountain. But he seems to have participated in the prestige of being a doctor, including the increased salary, by not correcting false references to his academic credentials.

In a sense Fountain is continuing in the modern world an old tribal tradition in some tribal groups for individuals to declare their identities. If a large number of people believed it, then it was so until ridicule caused one to change. In traditional tribal cultures there is much to be said for a system of credibility based on constituencies, but in contemporary societies it seems necessary to enforce standards of professionalism to protect the public and the profession. Modern standards, the emphasis on experts, however, have taken some of the fun out of tribal trickeries and pretensions.

Silence.

Doc Fountain stopped to talk with some admirers, near the statue of a warrior in the park. He looked up and said: "The tribes are invisible in the white world," and unbuttoned his vest. He smiled and returned to his visions and the tribal secrets of the earth park where he learned to sleep so well.

Sorrie and Fountain reached for the earth.

Sorrie Permission poked the trash.

Peter Fountain was an earthdiver, but not an earthdiver as his tribal ancestors had been. In the cities an imaginative tribal mixedblood must be an earthdiver to survive.

The Decembers

> Religious man thirsts for being. . . . This is as much as to say that religious man can live only in a sacred world, because it is only in such a world that he participates in being, that he has a real existence. . . . His terror of the chaos that surrounds his inhabited world corresponds to his terror of nothingness.
>
> Mircea Eliade, *The Sacred and the Profane*

Solomon December is an artist who paints tribal people.

Solomon is remembered as December, the realist painter from the reservation who sells his watercolors in barber shops in the suburbs. He never finished art school. He is an instinctive artist, a shaman with a brush, and his work has been named new tribal realism.

December works at the kitchen table, his studio.

The theme of most of his watercolors is labor, tribal people at work with strong arms and necks, and with round blithe faces that seem connected to the earth and water. New tribal realism is the critical matter that gives verbal meaning to those who admire the tribal people he celebrates in watercolors. December is not burdened with a vengeance or political trash in his art, and he offers no guilt images or racist properties.

December wrinkles his nose and smacks his fists together over the language of art criticism, but he does have a weakness for the critics of art criticism, the reversal. For example, he is forever quoting from *The Painted Word* by Tom Wolfe. Last week, in fact, he was in the local barber shop when a retired railroad agent asked him what one of his paintings meant. December leaned back, looked at his watercolor painting of tribal people tapping maple sugar trees, and quoted from *The Painted Word:*

"All these years. . . . I had assumed that, in art, if nowhere else, seeing is believing. . . . Well—how very short sighted. . . . I had gotten it backwards all along. Not 'seeing is believing,' you ninny, but 'believing is seeing.' "

Charlee Fairbanks December cooks and cleans and dreams while her husband, the watercolor shaman, as she calls him, hunkers over his work at the kitchen table between meals. Several small brushes are mounted between his fingers, with four racks of watercolors at his side.

The three rooms in their small suburban apartment, their clothes, the threadbare cotton carpet from a discount store, even the used television set, take on the solid tribal scent of boiled dinners. Wild rice, whole potatoes, walleye pike, and moose or venison. But she is not a tribal servant, a mere traditional throwback or housewife tied to the kitchen. Rather, she too is an artist; the kitchen table is also her table for more than food. The two share their idealized energies in art. He tells those who admire his work, even his critics, that his watercolors would not be possible without the imagination of his wife. He signs all of his paintings *decembers,* lowercase letters, plural.

Charlee imagines scenes while her husband paints them at the kitchen table. Her perceptual power is no accident. Her mother is a shaman, a dreamer, and a tribal healer on the reservation; Charlee has a powerful vision and has been trained as a water dowser.

Solomon December, she tells those who will listen, is the first man she saw with an aura, a blue radiance around his head and chest, and she trusted his unusual energies. The two first met on the reservation, during the summer. Solomon built and delivered small wooden boxes to Charlee, who covered the bottoms with ice chips and then moved the boxes down the line to be filled with fresh reservation fish. The boxes were shipped to the cities.

The first time he stepped through the door she saw his light and has been with him ever since. She knew he was an artist even before he knew he could paint watercolors. Their love, and the small movements in their world, are ceremonies too private to be revealed, too intimate to be told. The two tribal realists in the kitchen are dedicated to their mixedblood tribal families, generous to their friends, and cordial to strangers. To write about them one must start with *one* watercolor painting, two tribal fishermen in a boat, for example, and then move backward in time through each minute touch and line of color the artist makes at the kitchen table.

"It is not so much a fault or bad manners," Charlee said to the two scholars as she trimmed the burner flame under the moose stew, "but the embarrassment and the pleasure he feels from a loud fart in public. . . . He tells people he is clapping over a good meal, and then he points to me . . . *me,* the embarrassed one looking the other way."

Solomon December is an artist by vision and experience, not by social manners or class conscious vengeance. His art is a celebration of families. The realism is idealized from an urban perspective of tribal people at work. The figures in his paintings gather wild rice, catch fish, repair automobiles, and cut pulpwood, laborers, all dressed in common working clothes, not feathers and beads. Charlee imagines December in his figures, and he finds himself there, in the realism of human labor, but he has not painted an artist at work on a kitchen table.

At a recent special exhibition of four tribal painters, December and three abstract artists, at the Minneapolis Regional Native American Center, two visiting scholars raved about the realism in his watercolors.

December, best known by his last name alone, was admired in tribal families and by art critics and historians, but such enthusiastic praise at a public exhibition was unusual. The two scholars were Russian professors on a special tour from the Gorky Institute of World Literature in Moscow, and with no hesitation they avoided the work of the abstract painters. In loud voices the two scholars named Solomon December the Jack London of the tribal watercolor.

Charlee saved December from silence. She remembered the *Call of the Wild* and several other popular novels by the adventure writer which she had read in mission boarding schools. "The first thing we learned from the old nuns, of course, is that he was a socialist and a spiritual primitive."

"Of course," said the thin scholar.

"I would rather be ashes than dust," said the stout scholar, quoting Jack London from a newspaper interview. He gestured toward the watercolors on the wall as he spoke. "The proper function of man is to live, not exist. I shall not waste my days in trying to prolong them," he quoted from London.

"Your work lives in labor," said the thin scholar, "as passion endures in words and reason."

"One can feel your work as one feels the earth," said the stout scholar. The Russions were most interested in literature. The thin professor studied tribal literature and art, and the stout scholar was an expert on Jack London and the literature of realism. But both were pleased to view and discuss art with tribal artists, as a means, the two scholars said, of better understanding tribal consciousness and imagination. What the two scholars found unusual was the relative absence of realism in tribal art and literature. There was much that seemed surreal, metaphysical, spiritual, abstract, but little realism.

At a recent lecture on *Histrionics in Modern Art,* December remembered that the speaker quoted from *The Painted Word* by Tom Wolfe, who was inspired to write his book when he read a review on an exhibition of seven realists. Later, December found the book and memorized several passages. The critic wrote that "realism does not lack its partisans, but it does rather conspicuously lack a persuasive theory."

December did not look at the two scholars while he searched his memories for the right words to recite from Tom Wolfe. When he remembered, he looked up and smiled. "Literary became a code word for all that seemed hopelessly retrograde about realistic art. . . ."

December quoted Wolfe with obvious pleasure: "The idea was that half the power of realistic painting comes from the sentiments the viewer hauls along to it, like so much mental baggage. . . . *and so much mental refuse,* Tom Wolfe should have added."

"We could not withhold our enthusiasm for your work," said the thin scholar, clapping his hands in front of each watercolor.

"Why so little realism?" asked the stout scholar.

"Because we are *not* real," said December, remembering an interview in the *New Mexico Magazine* with R.C. Gorman. "The interviewer was asking him about tribal identities, and Gorman, who paints tribal women in beautiful desert tones, said *I wish people would quit pushing my being Indian.*"

Gorman: "Fritz Scholder is better at it than I ever was. . . ."

Interviewer: "Why don't you chuck the headband. . . . the image?"

Gorman: "What, and go bald like the white man?"

"Later, in an interview published in *Artlines,*" December continued, "Lisa Sherman asked Fritz Scholder, *What do you think are the greatest misconceptions that people have about you?*

"First of all," Scholder said, "that I'm an Indian artist. Another thing that disappoints me is the criticism that, in one way or another, I've sold out. That idea makes me feel very sad, because if there's one thing I've never done in my whole life, it is sell out. . . . There will always be those who will hate, those who will be confused, and those who will love you."

December turned toward his watercolors.

The Russians compared his watercolor of the tribal fisherman with a bright-colored oil painting of an Indian head on a citrus fruit reamer on a mesa at dusk. "This appears to be a *real* reamer, but what does it mean in tribal experience?" asked the stout scholar.

Charlee smiled and then introduced the artist who painted the citrus reamer. The artist was either nervous or irritated, but he did explain with small finger gestures, unusual for such a huge canvas, that "this here *reamer* is a symbolic *reamer* of the white world, fresh orange juice and all, and the white man has crowned our sacred mesas with his secular *reamer*. . . . the white man stuck it to us, but the Indian head will ride to the end."

"Of course," said the thin scholar, "reason over passion."

"We have much to learn," said the stout scholar.

"Are there mesas where you live?"

"No, not for real," said the artist, pulling his hands down his braids. "No, I lived in New York City, and came out here to go to art school . . . everywhere else the fuckin whites tell us what to paint and how to paint."

December farted, a well-timed low applause, followed by two short whistles. Perfect timing, the touch of a tribal trickster and realist at a moment in the unreal. The fart relieved the humor in the scholars, a peasant humor in the stout scholar.

Later, at the informal reception, the scholars were treated to tribal stories, satire, hostilities, and, some ridicule, which was never too far from the rim of serious racism and cultural apposition.

"What would your government do about the violence of the Red Lake Reservation?" an artist asked the two scholars who were involved in a comparative discussion about beer.

"We are common people, not the government."

"Would your government send troops in to settle the differences, or what?" The abstract artist was intense. He continued questioning the scholars. "Or would you let the skins kill themselves?"

"We lack that imagination."

"How about other nations your government has invaded?" The citrus reamer artist joined the interrogation. "Tribal people are no different, would you invade our reservations?"

"We are common people," said the stout scholar, "we would never come to this place or to your home unless we were invited, perhaps we should leave now."

"Not for a minute," said Charlee, sweeping her arms around the scholars as if they were children and leading them from the reception. "You are invited to have dinner at our house with no talk about violence."

December chauffeured the scholars in his reservation car with slogans attached to the trunk, doors, and side panels. The clutch was too thin for subtle starts. The lurch from the parking lot startled the scholars.

"Indian car," said Charlee.

"None better, in the worst of health we can make it back to the reservation," said December. He turned right down Franklin Avenue to show the scholars the urban reservation.

"In that house," said December, pointing to a building with four small units, "at one time there were four families, more than thirty-six skins in all, living there. . . . little skins were stacked in the cupboards."

"Indians are charged more for dumps than decent housing," said Charlee, "which is why we live in the suburbs."

"What is a skin?"

"Indian, whole or fair skin."

December turned down Chicago Avenue, stopped in front of Dolly's Tavern, where he told stories about the oral traditions at the bar, "a kind of tribal bulletin board on foot," and then continued through the downtown and toward the north suburbs.

"We live in Coon Rapids."

"Could you tell us some of your thoughts about the Native American Center," said the thin scholar. "We wondered, so expensive a building, and the people are still so poor, the homes around do not seem good places to live."

"Ronald Libertus is the name to remember," said Charlee. "He's from the Leech Lake Reservation, a person who works hard and gets too little credit or praise. Well, he had a good plan way back before the center was built. He proposed that we use the millions it would take to build an architectural monument like the Native American Center to buy all the buildings along Franklin Avenue for several blocks. . . . His idea was to buy the street that skins lived on and make it an urban reservation marketplace, a place where people could develop their own ideas about economics, arts, and services, a sort of tribal cooperative that would bring money into the community rather than send it out all the time, like reservations. But the professionals, all the experts, the urban planners, and white architects, made a monument for their civilization, not ours."

"The monument has been nothing but trouble," said December. "It is a beautiful meeting place, tribal people find friends and good things there, but the politics are a disaster."

"What do you mean, the politics?" asked the thin scholar.

"Let me tell you one story because it is hard for me to talk about the troubles," said December, leaning back to gesture to the two scholars who were sitting in the back seat. "Several years ago, a skin who worked at the center, who had a reputation for having light fingers, wanted to get into a room where expensive film and video equipment was stored. Because so much equipment had been stolen, the curator of the museum who was in charge of the equipment changed the locks. There were only two keys to the room; the curator and the skin each had one. Well, the equipment continued to disappear so the curator changed the locks again but kept the keys. One night, the skin tried to get into the room. When his key did not work, he got angry and took an ax and chopped down this beautiful ten-foot-tall solid cedar wood door. The door fell, he took what he needed, and then to cover his crime he removed a door from a room on the other side of the building and put it on the equipment room. Next day, the curator came in and discovered that his key did not work in the door. Then someone found the felled door in the basement, and the story came together. The curator approached the skin with the information. Now listen to this," said December over his shoulder, "the skin said he did indeed chop down the door, like the village during the war, he did in the door to save it. . . . He laughed, but no one else did, and the curator moved on to work in a place that made more sense."

"You are right, who would believe it?"

"Too many stories," said December, as he turned into the large parking lot behind their apartment complex. "Since we moved in here and got our last name on a parking place, several other people asked for name plates for the months. New trend, parking by the month name. See, over there are the other winter months."

Over wild rice, squash, and moose stew, the scholars discussed their families, their travels, dreams, and experiences. The scholars told about people, the earth, and labor, but not politics. The stout scholar, a peasant horseman, told stories about the earth in a language of remembrance. The thin scholar, whose father was a doctor, told stories about people and their behavior.

"We noticed," said the thin scholar, "so many paintings of Indian heads, abstract and what seem to be traditional motifs. . . . Do people demand these Indian heads?"

"High prices for Indian heads," December answered. "Much

higher than prices for other art. . . . Private collectors like them, seems traditional to them, but wooden Indians are wooden Indians."

"Why is that?"

"Scalping in the arts."

"Scalping?"

"Tribal art with a vengeance," December explained. "Some abstract artists make a fortune selling feathered Indian heads to whites. . . . Indian heads are dead Indian pictures, wooden nickel faces, cigar store poses; the abstract Indian is the perfect victim for the racist liberal, and the Indian head artist returns the invented cigar store image with a vengeance."

"It *is* true," said the stout scholar, "Indian heads are most popular with the Germans. . . . They have so many Indian organizations there, perhaps because Karl May wrote so many stories about Winnitou, adventures of the invented Apache warrior."

"How do you mean vengeance?"

"Indian heads are commercials for the refurbished past, not the *real* tribal past, but the colonial artifact past when the white elite bought whole tribes and sacred vestments for wall decorations. . . . The artist sells the image that most appeals to the new colonialists; the racist wants his own Indian head in a new color code. . . . Some artists sell Indian heads to whites with a vengeance in the same way elitist artists have been selling electronic white noise music to museums in small towns."

The stout scholar leaned forward to ask the artist to show them his studio. "We would be so pleased to see where you do your painting. . . . I am especially interested in the actual place where painters and writers do their work."

"Here, you are in it, this is my studio," said December, a wide smile turning on his face. He expanded his arms a fathom to include the whole kitchen as his small studio.

"December loves to eat and loves to paint," Charlee said in humor. She passed the wild rice around the table one more time and explained that "he eats and paints in the same place, at the table."

"Wonderful, wonderful, a real artist," exclaimed the stout scholar. He presented a small bottle from his inside pocket, and filled four small glasses with vodka.

"Now we must toast the *real* artist, the art of realism whose works are his real work."

December whistled and then smiled.

The stout scholar rolled several times the vodka and the name December over his tongue. "December, December, December, tell me December, what is the meaning of your name, besides the month of course?"

"And if you would," added the thin scholar, "tell us how or where you learned to paint . . . please?"

"The people in my paintings are at work, their work is good, their work makes me feel good," December explained, "and this conversation about them is important. No throwbacks to the way the white man locks us up in traditional inventions, no need for vengeance in my work, the people are connected to the earth. . . .

"December is the month of my birth, the winter solstice, and the time to begin telling stories. My grandfather was a teller of fine stories, and so named for the time. When the missionaries came around to translate his name for the white colonialists, his nickname *manidoo gizisoons,* which means *moon of the spirits,* was translated as his last name."

December appeals to socialists and some workers because he idealizes workers in a tribal cultures, rather than painting artifact warriors with a vengeance for bourgeois patrons. While some tribal artists capture masculine warriors on horses and in canoes for the prisoners of wealth, December shows tribal people catching fish, building houses, gathering wild rice, turning arrows, and working with the earth for survival. Museums have defined Indians as leisure artifacts, and demand that their faces from the past be separated from common labor. The artists who separate the real tribal world from their abstract Indian heads do it with a vengeance.

"My hands work for the tribal people who work," said December. "Some white heads surround themselves with Indian heads. . . . The world is made with heads and hands.

"I never graduated from art school, even though I went there for a few quarters. There are good tribal people working there, but schools never did much for me," said December. He seemed apologetic, some need to explain his resistance to an institution that measures the world in credits and degrees. "Schools stole my imagination and my energies to see the real world in my painting. . . . I know how to paint, I have a special way of seeing the world, what I needed was time to work, a time to work at my art, *not my manners.* I was an artist and had little time to waste on insecure teachers who would have me painting abstract Indian heads."

December served the two scholars a special chokecherry wine which he and Charlee make each year, enough for themselves and for special visitors.

Charlee traveled through the color of the wine when it was poured. She traveled from the first summers on the reservation, to four art schools in several cities, and then, in time, to his real work in watercolors. She shared his vision, and when he paints at the kitchen table, she feels his hands. Her vision and memories move with his in color. She becomes his artist, she concentrates her imagination to his work, their work, and she shares the pleasures and pains of their creation. She knows him to be an unusual tribal person.

"Patrick Des Jarlait never painted problems, or Indian heads for a vengeance. He loved the working image of the tribe, and he had no need to hate or to present people as victims." Tears rolled down his cheeks when he spoke of his friend and teacher who had died of cancer. "Des Jarlait did not consider himself a traditionalist even though he was born and lived for a time on the reservation. . . . He was not interested in the flat tones of the southwest tribal artist. Des Jarlait painted tribal people who worked their way from the canvas into your heart and imagination. People look at his work and feel comfortable with the artist, the viewers become artists in his work. No one was separated from the earth or from familiar places. . . . He gave so much, I think. . . . We loved him, and he and my wife inspired me to work in my own vision."

"When we were first married, Des Jarlait invited us to his house once; we were so excited and embarrassed," Charlee said. "When we got there we were so comfortable because he and his wife lived like real people. We knew them just like his work, and we knew we could be artists too because we learned that we never had to learn how to live *like* an artist. . . . We learned that we would *be* artists.

"December works like Des Jarlait did, he paints at the kitchen table, a comfortable place for families and workers, where we all sit when we feel good together. . . . A place of oral traditions. Studios are for people who paint Indian heads for a vengeance."

The Russians drank chokecherry wine and told stories about farm families, characters from literature, the ocean, but never a word about spies and political intrigues.

The stout scholar farted.

EARTHDIVERS AT THE INDIAN CENTER

The Sociodowser

> The influence medicine men exert in tribal Indian societies can hardly be overemphasized. The medicine man cures the sick, he reveals things hidden in time and space, leads ceremonies and rites, and is in many places the foremost authority on the traditions of the tribe. His supernatural equipment enables him to secure the success of the economy of the group through magic and other ritual activity.
>
> Åke Hultkrantz, *The Religions of the American Indians*

Father Bearald One rolled back in the clover, spread his arms wide behind his head, stared through the flashing poplar leaves, and pictured in his mind the semitrailer truck that contained the two tribal vans impounded by the state revenue commissioner.

The ignition switches were pulled at high noon, while the drivers were at lunch, the wires were crossed, and then the tribal vans were impounded for unpaid taxes and driven under guard into a wide aluminum trailer and stored at a secret location.

Father Bearald One, a well-known shaman dowser and urban trickster, was summoned to locate, through his visions and intuitive memories, the place where the tribal vans were stored. Bearald One is neither a priest nor a church celebrant, but he bears the honorific name because he wears the black clothes and collar of a cleric.

Tragedies and ironies, with a dash of woodland tribal chance, influence the best of families and no less determine the successes and failures of tribal organizations. The Prospect Park American Indian Center, dedicated to social service, education, and the balance of cultural anxieties on the urban reservation, purchased the vans with federal funds to transport tribal enrollees to and from a special industrial education program in precision optics. The vans, however, were used for personal business most of the time. On the side, the drivers operated as short-haul movers, and several nights a week the vans became limousines. For spiritual favors and small cash fees tribal families were chauffeured to bingo games at the center. Games of chance were connections to moccasin games in the traditional tribal past, fashions of mythic survival in the woodland, but the cash flowed unaccounted, ironies overburdened the games, taxes on bingo profits went unpaid, chance failed, and the red limousines were impounded.

"But we are sovereign, man," said a member of the center board at a meeting that afternoon. "No one, man, no one can take our vans like that. . . ."

"The state did, man, stole them," said another board member.

"New treaties on wheels," said a board member dressed in a black and blue ribbon shirt and a summer suit. The scars on his right cheek twitched from time to time, raising the corner of his lips.

"White racists invented taxes. . . ."

"Give us back our land and our vans," said a small tribal woman perched on the back of a chair near the oval conference table. She invented tribal enemies in the room and spoke to them in a loud voice. "No white *man* can take our wheels, we have a natural right to turn our wheels on mother earth. . . . No *man* can steal our right to move as tribal women."

"We have treaties on wheels."

"We got a right to our vans."

"This is war, man, war, the tribal van war."

"We need a shaman," said the board member in the black and blue ribbon shirt, as he removed his suit coat and walked in wide circles around the conference table. The corner of his lips on the right side of his face lifted between words.

"No, not a shaman, we got enough troubles."

"We need a shaman to find where the vans are hidden so *we*

can steal them back," said the man in the ribbon shirt. "No law on stealing back our own vans."

"Shamans are weirdies."

"Who cares, when we turn him on the white man."

"We need our vans back, weird or not."

"Nothing is the same now," said the board member in the black and blue ribbon shirt. He continued his wide circle around the conference table. "Our wheels are gone, and we could lose the whole place without our bingo limousines."

The center was more like a colonial fort dependent on federal funds, than a place for visions and dreams in the new tribal urban world. The vans were hitched to the transportation of enrollees in industrial education, the official purpose, and the enrollees were direct connections to funds that paid the salaries of several board members. To lose the vans was to lose the federal funds; salaries, members of the center board, and most important, bingo games, would fall in turn like ripe rows of wild rice.

"We got our pride."

"Pride is for fools who are too scared to steal," said the imperfect fool in the black and blue ribbon shirt. "What we got to keep is the cash flow, remember the cash flow, from the bingo games."

"You sound like a priest, man."

"Great idea."

"What?"

"The shaman. . . ."

"Who?"

"Father Bearald One."

"The fake priest?"

"Better than some real ones."

"Bearald is strange."

"Strange is what we need."

"Bearald finds people, solves crimes, calls animals, and he even does strange things in court, man, he can cause people to think they are really innocent," said the pacer in the black and blue ribbon shirt. Perspiration rolled down his forehead. Wide wet circles expanded under his arms on his shirt. "The best shaman make me the most nervous," he said, and then he told several stories about the mixedblood urban shaman dowser.

INDIAN CIRCLE CIRCLE

The Minnesota Chippewa Tribe, said the man in the black and blue ribbon shirt, drawing a deep breath to begin his stories, once upon a time sponsored a special summer education program for tribal high school students at the Chippewa Ranch on the White Earth Reservation. The idea, believe it or not, was to think tribal and be tribal with federal funds, he said, walking in a wide circle with his head tilted backward, in fact the proposed purpose was to learn and practice how to be a real noble savage in the woodland.

Well, the rabbit and her shit hit the intake fans when the students and counselors, more than a hundred all together, from dozens of different reservations, drank a few beers and danced around a fire like well brushed skins. The students got to dancing and feeling real good when an administrator blew the whistle on what she thought was a war dance fever and called in local white investigators.

Meanwhile, said the man in the black and blue ribbon shirt, on the western side of his wide circle, Father Bearald One was visiting Shaman Newcrows, grandson of the famous tribal psychotaxidermist, who lived back in the woods near the Chippewa Ranch.

Well, Bearald and Newcrows were awakened, as in a distant tribal dream, to the sound of old-time singing, and the drum, the sound of the drum from thunderstorms crashing through the bodies on the wind. The two shaman dowsers moved through the brush and across the meadows with *jiibayag,* tribal spirits, toward the sound of the drum. When they reached the fire the two shamans danced with the students in the circle. No one was surprised; it seemed right that the drum would summon dancers and spirits on the wind from the dark woods.

Later, the students gathered around the fire, said the man in the black and blue ribbon shirt, while Newcrows told stories about his grandfather the shaman psychotaxidermist who, according to his vision, brought a whole world of animals and birds back to life in a thunderstorm on a four hole golf course, the first in the state, and was arrested for "animule molestation."

District Court Judge Silas Bandied snapped his ceramic teeth in the hollow downtown courtroom and cleared his throat three times, his religious trine, like a cormorant coughing up three fat goldfish.

"The evidence is clear that you were dressed in a bear animule mask rapacious sight that it must have been that night on our new golf course," said Bandied, but when he cleared his throat to begin again he was interrupted.

"Ceremonial bear, not a mask," said the grandson, quoting his grandfather Shaman Newcrows, who was leaning back in his chair at a comfortable escape distance from the judge and the prosecutor, dressed in a red velvet suit with a bear claw necklace.

"Shaman Newcrows, my grandfather, was born on the shores of Bad Medicine Lake on the White Earth Reservation, and blessed with animal spirits and avian visions. He traveled in magical flight through four levels of consciousness and the underworld and learned the languages of animals and birds."

"What, if anything, can this savage evildoer know about bears and animules?" asked the judge. He leaned down behind his massive dark bench to scratch his ankles and did not hear the prosecutor read from *Bear Ceremonialism in the Northern Hemisphere* by A. Irving Hallowell:

"The categories of rational thought, by which we are accustomed to separate human life from animal life and the supernatural from the natural, are drawn upon lines which the facts of primitive cultures do not fit.

"Animals are believed to have essentially the same sort of animating agency which man possesses. They have a language of their own, can understand what human beings say and do, have forms of social or tribal organization, and live a life which is parallel in other respects to that of human societies."

"Where did those tics come from?" the judge asked as he emerged from behind the bench. He pulled his black robe over his head and scratched at his thighs, shoulders, and crotch.

"From the bears," explained the breathless prosecutor, scratching at his cheeks. "Bear tics trained to disrupt our system of justice."

"That savage evildoer did this to us. . . ."

"Drop the charges," wailed the prosecutor while he scratched with both hands at his crotch. "Drop the goddamn charges and call the tics off. . . ."

"Shaman Newcrows the psychotaxidermist waited with a wide smile on his face," said his grandson, at the fire, "and watched tribal trained bear tics attack the court."

"Charges dismissed!" screamed the judge from the floor behind his bench where he was scratching and scratching like a reservation mongrel on a tic mound.

"My grandfather whistled four times on the wind, and in seconds the bear tics were gone and the prosecutor and the judge were back at their benches and chairs with their forms and robes and pencils and plurals."

The fire leaped from face to face in the darkness.

WILD RICE REFUGE REFUGE

Father Bearald One told stories, said the board member in the black and blue ribbon shirt, about the time his tribal friends from the reservation appeared in federal court in a dispute over the regulation of wild rice on the Rice Lake Wildlife Refuge in Minnesota, and testified in their own tribal language:

Charles Aubid, an *anishinaabe* man in his eighties, was the first witness. When United States District Judge Miles Lord, formerly the State Attorney General, raised his right hand, attempting to show the witness how to take the oath, the witness smiled and *waved* back at Lord, determined to know no more than he chose to know in the oral tradition of his tribal language.

Lord and the witness waved at each other and the visitors waved at each other in an unusual burst of courtroom humor. Most of the people in the courtroom were tribal people, elders, from the reservation.

The oath was read in translation by George Aubid and Florence Barber, which pleased the witness. He smiled, a wide smile spreading the loose skin on his narrow thin face, and when he turned, his dark eyes seemed four times larger through the thick lenses on his glasses. It was the first time in our memories that the oath was read in the *anishinaabe* language.

The tribal elders, including Sam Yankee, and others from Mille Lacs and East Lake, were in court to stop the federal government from regulating the natural wild rice harvest on the refuge, which was on tribal land.

Shaman Newcrows was there in the courtroom, and together we concentrated on our tribal language in the oral tradition. White people, even the federal attorneys, stammered and hesitated, but the tribal people there spoke our language in clear and powerful voices.

Later, during recess, we also turned loose a few bear tics on the officers of the court just to be sure that our voice was heard.

Charles Aubid, through his son as an interpreter, asked the judge who hired him to be a judge over tribal wild rice rights. Lord turned and wheeled in his official chair down behind the bench closer to the witness and, through the interpreter, asked the old man with wide eyes if he could understand that both the "Congress and the President of the United States appointed me" to be a federal judge.

"Damn right I do," Aubid said in English.

We were all surprised.

Lord seemed to leap from his chair in humor at the words, he rolled down the bench on his chair in laughter, even the somber federal clerks and court officers were able to smile, and when he recovered the judge rolled back near the witness and said, "now let's try it without the interpreter."

"All right," said Aubid.

"You may proceed then."

"What did you hear about the regulation of wild rice on the refuge?" the witness was asked. The judge explained that he did not think his court had jurisdiction but he was eager and willing to listen to the dispute between tribal people and the federal government over the wild rice harvest.

Charles Aubid testified that he heard old John Squirrel, an important man on the reservation, talking with a government man before the refuge was established by the federal government.

"The government man said we could retain control of the rice harvest," he said through his son the interpreter. Aubid chose to continue answering questions in his tribal language because it was the language of his visual memories.

The federal attorney objected to his testimony.

"Squirrel is dead," Lord told Aubid, "and you can't say what a dead man said." Lord explained the rules that limited testimonies and information to the experiences of each witness. Aubid, seldom cornered in word wars, pointed out that what he remembered about old John Squirrel was no different than what the judge remembered from law books and voices in old cases.

Charles Aubid looked around the federal courtroom in silence. His enormous eyes seemed to glow, like the eyes of an animal caught in the light at the treeline. He raised his withered right hand and cupped it behind his ear, as if he were singing at the drum, and then he spoke in a loud voice.

"Lord, why should I believe what a white man says when you don't believe what John Squirrel said," said Aubid through his son the interpreter.

Lord smiled and laced his hands on the bench.

DOWSING THE STUDENTS

Father Bearald One influenced the students and counselors to open each moment of their interior tensions and glories, like flowers on the meadow, trees in the wind, animals in winter, and smile with the pleasures of personal control as a warrior. Bearald taught the students to meditate and dowse, how to summon the biomagnetic tribal energies realized through visual connections to the earth. Some students trusted their visions and new energies more than others, but together one morning the students turned from their food like birds in magical flight.

Will Rogers, Jr., a high-paid consultant on a public relations tour for the Bureau of Indian Affairs, visited Indian Circle Circle and told stories over breakfast about his father and other mixed-blood pantribal skins. Few were there to listen because the students turned in silence and staged a hunger strike. To begin with, the food was poor—not a significant nutritional loss to miss a few meals—but the students were also critical of the administration of the program and followed their hunger strike with a formal meeting with the elected officials of the Minnesota Chippewa Tribe.

The students and counselors were serious, and in the warrior tradition told tribal officials about the problems in the program. Their information was personal, factual, not rumor. The staff and teachers, rumor bound for the most part, did not seem to believe in the fundamental principles of teaching tribal students to be honest and independent.

The director and his assistants seemed defensive, as separated administrators seem to be, and at the end of the meeting the tribal officials fired the staff and reorganized the program, according to the values and needs of the students. One administrator refused to leave the building. He said he wanted to stay in the program as a student.

"I want to learn how to be an Indian," he told a reporter, "and participate in the program and classes."

Bearald One smiled and turned a stone in his right hand.

BLUE BEARALD IN THE BRUSH

Father Bearald One was born in the brush on the shore of Long Lost Lake on the White Earth Reservation. His mother, a mixedblood from the reservation, never revealed who his father was, but rumors abounded in the brush when Bearald One, her first child, took to wearing the clothes of a priest when he was thirteen and in the seventh grade at a federal boarding school on the reservation.

"That savage knows who he is and what he wears," said a white teacher at the school. The rumors implied that the priesthood and the dark clothes of a cleric were genetic. No surprise, because the white teacher also believed that tribal children were retarded and incapable of rational thought.

"Savagism out on the line," she said.

Bearald One was a strange child; he heard voices and visited distant places in his dreams. He followed bluebirds in his visions, his guardian avian spirit, and he trembled like a bird with pneumatic bones, from time to time at different places. He found a poplar stick cleaned by a beaver which became his dowsing rod. Soon, tribal people came to him and asked him to find lost people and places. The white people on the reservation asked the young shaman, in secret sessions, to cure various phobias. He cured one white school teacher of acarophobia, or the fear of insects, and another of auroraphobia, or fear of the northern lights.

When he was four years old he trembled while picking berries with his mother and other tribal families. He climbed up on top of a large round rock with other children, and there he began to tremble and twitch. At first his mother feared that he was possessed with evil, but when she discovered that the trembling came from the rock and from other places and energies, she knew he had a strange power over the world. Later, when he had demonstrated his abilities to find lost people and places on the reservation, she told stories about how her stomach had been surrounded with a pale blue aura several weeks before he was born. She said she remembered how blue the room seemed when he was born; the doctors and nurses at the public health hospital even commented on the unusual color in the room. Some people thought that the blue color that surrounded him was caused by the weather, by the approach of a thunderstorm.

When he was twelve he envisioned the bluebird and learned to speak the languages of birds. Later, when he practiced the arts of healing and dowsing with an old shaman who lived alone in the woods, he learned to speak the languages of bears and beavers, and three trees, the poplar, cedar, and white pine.

BLUE BEARALD ON THE BOARD

Father Bearald One became better known on urban reservations as a map dowser, a tribal sensitive, a shaman dowser, a water and spirit witch, and a healer and medicine man. He has traveled in his dreams with bears, and because he is the first in his family to possess such powers he was named the number *one.* His friends in boarding school determined his honorific nickname. Bearald is his sacred dream name.

Father Bearald pictured in his mind the two impounded tribal vans and the aluminum semitrailer. He rolled over on his stomach in the clover, opened a street map of the cities, and with the tip of his finger on the right hand he moved across the map from west to east in ritual arcs as the sun from season to season in secular reversals, until his finger stopped and trembled. Then he turned the map on the side, still picturing in his mind the vans and the trailer, and moved his finger in slow motion arcs from top to bottom until his finger stopped and trembled a second time. There, at an intersection on the map, at the international airport, the old tribal map dowser had located where the vans were impounded and stored.

"Bullshit, at the airport?"

"Maybe the bastards flew them out."

"Finger on a map, shit man, what is this crap? We want our vans back, man, not some beartrap at the end of a runway," said the manager of the bingo operations.

"One sure way to find out," said the board member in the sweat stained black and blue ribbon shirt. "Me and the shaman will check this out, meanwhile the rest of you work out a plan to snatch the vans back tonight."

The red vans were there, at the intersection where his finger trembled, stored in an abandoned airplane hanger. That night the shaman focused his energies on the night watchperson, causing her to be distracted and becalmed at the gate, while the board members, dressed in full ceremonial vestments, an urban warrior contradance, drove their vans over two ramps coupled at the top of the fence behind the hanger.

Thrilled with their success in finding the vans, the board provided free transportation to the center for a celebration dance and two free bingo cards.

The next morning, Father Bearald with the board member in the black and blue ribbon shirt found their own hiding place for the vans on the second floor of a carriage house. The drivers installed loud sirens that would sound if the vans were tampered with. When not in use, the vans were stored at the carriage house. Several weeks passed before the state commissioner of revenue was informed that the vans were missing. He ordered a search of the center, and with the appropriate court orders, he was allowed to question the drivers and board members. Whenever the state revenue agents were in the center, Father Bearald One was there, focusing his shamanic energies to becalm the investigators. The commissioner assigned different investigators from time to time because so little information was gathered from the interviews. The becalmed investigators asked simple questions about the weather, families, and social events.

"Man, that shaman is weird," said a van driver.

"What we need are a few weird shamans on the board," said the ersatz warrior in the black and blue ribbon shirt. "Listen, this shaman did good, and we should vote him in and take him on the board. . . . No shit, man."

Bearald One was elected to serve on the board of directors but not without questions and some harsh criticism from those who did not trust or believe in spiritual power and shamanism.

"Man, he never says nothing."

"Man, you have been away from the reservation too long," said the board member in the black and blue ribbon shirt.

"I don't trust him."

"Why?"

"My guts tell me, that's why."

"What?"

"He's too strange. . . . like no skin I ever knew."

"What's strange about him?"

"His foot, how about his foot?"

"His foot has nothing to do with being on the board," responded the man in the black and blue ribbon shirt. "You got a twisted nose, what does that mean?"

"No, I mean he walks like a witch doctor; least he could do is wear a shoe or something. . . . What's under that overshoe?"

"You are weird."

"That foot bothers me too."

"Then you should invite him in and ask him about his foot, and if his story is good enough we can take him on the board."

"Bring him in. . . ."

"Yeah, man, bring the weird one in."

Father Bearald One was invited to the next board meeting in two weeks time. He waited in the lounge, erect on an orange chair which turned his blue radiance into a peculiar green, outside the board room. The chairman of the board, the one in the black and blue ribbon shirt, called the shaman dowser in and directed him to a swivel chair at the end of the large oval conference table. The board members looked down at their papers and fingers as the shaman passed their chairs, avoiding his eyes as did so many people who sensed, but did not understand, his power. Some believed that the shaman has the power to cause people to avert their eyes. The shaman controls who looks at him to spare his energies. Bearald was a shaman with a clear vision, a person who serves communities, not a visitor from the darkness, white streams of evil, but his sensitivities were misunderstood, most often by those who had something to hide or someone to fear.

"Mister One," said the chairman in the black and blue ribbon shirt, "we have considered you as a future board member, but before we vote on new members we want to ask a few questions."

"There are more answers than questions," said the map dowser shaman as he settled into the overstuffed chair and leaned back to admire the fabricated environment. "Perhaps you could give me a few answers and see if I have some questions."

"Who will begin?"

"The earth is flat," said the shaman.

Silence.

The board members looked down at their hands.

"Someone should have a question?"

Silence.

"Anyone with an answer?"

Silence.

The chairman sat in silence for several minutes and then nodded to Father Bearald One that the meeting had ended. Bearald smiled and while he was walking toward the door, a board member looked up in surprise as he passed and asked him about his deformed foot.

"What hit your foot?"

"A giant poplar tree," the shaman answered.

"What is that you wear on it now?"

"An overshoe."

"An overshoe?"

"A plain black rubber zipper overshoe."

"But this is summer."

"Best time, too cold in winter."

"Why an overshoe?"

"Nothing else fits so well."

"Let me see it."

"See what?"

"Your foot."

"No."

"No, never ask that," said the man in the black and blue ribbon shirt.

"Never?"

"No."

"Sure enough," said the shaman as he turned and sat down in a chair against the wall. But rather than showing his foot in the overshoe, he removed the shoe on his other foot, the normal foot, because no one specified which foot. Then he removed his sock and stretched and wriggled his angular toes in the direction of the board members.

The board members looked down again, avoiding first the gaze of the shaman dowser, and then avoiding his toes. One board member started to ask about his other foot, the crushed foot, but before the words formed a complete sentence he stammered and hesitated. The question to see his crushed foot was never asked, the board was becalmed, tongue-tied by the energies of the shaman dowser.

Father Bearald One became a board member, the vote was unanimous, but in a few weeks the harsh criticism and malevolent rumors dominated all references to him. Several board members became more suspicious of the shaman dowser, accused him of not supporting tribal ideals, accused him of being a witch, and blamed him for various problems that seemed to increase when he became a member of the board. The problems were there from the beginning, but it is important in tribal communities to attribute causation and blame to those who seem to have personal power.

"Like what?" asked the man in the black and blue ribbon shirt.

"Well, like one thing, the bingo games."

"What about them?"

"We lose money since he got on the board."

The cash prize decreases with the numbers called to complete the row and word *bingo*. The fewer numbers called, the greater the cash prize. The shaman was accused of influencing the numbers called in favor of certain people at the game.

True, Father Bearald did inspire the results of the game, which lessened the enormous cash profits to the center, but his influence was not self-serving. His energies were not effective but for the good. Bearald would stand at the entrance to the center on game nights and choose an old tribal person whose thoughts were revealed to him and whose needs he could feel. He would arrange to sit beside the tribal person during the game. He never played bingo to win himself, but to serve others. The tribal men and women he chose to win were people responsible for the care of others; their needs to win at bingo were to serve and care for others. Bearald could perceive the differences in people, those who cared for others and those whose needs to win were for mere selfish material gain. When the cage was turned and the numbers rolled, the shaman pictured the numbers and letters in his mind and concentrated on the numbers to complete a row in favor of the person he chose to win. Bingo, bingo, bingo, bingo, on the first six or seven numbers called, when the cash prize was the highest. Although the center lost some cash to higher prize awards, the numbers of people playing the game increased because of the excitement over so many winners of large cash prizes.

"Old Sophie won last week."

"What card did she have?"

"She needed it too."

"Where was she sitting, near here?"

"Winnie won the week before."

"She has all the grandchildren with her now."

"This is a special card."

"Bingo, *bingo,* bingo, bingo."

"What else?" asked the man in the black and blue ribbon shirt.

"Ever since he has been on the board we got nothin but troubles with the old ladies on the ride vans, nothin but bitchin. . . ."

"Bearald never rides with the women."

"Never mind, he's there somehow, doing something to the women. . . . I think he spooked em and now we got nothin but troubles."

"Like what?"

"Well, last night, when the driver stopped. . . . Well, you know, he stopped for a second, man. . . . The women took over the van and drove here on their own."

"So what?"

"So what? So, dipshit driver calls the cops and tells em the van is ripped off. . . . Next thing we could get the revenue people back, man."

"What else?"

"More?"

"All this goin on since that shaman asshole got on the board. He messed up on the fur trade last week."

"What fur trade?"

"Well, some skins were gonna trade off . . . knock off, a fur place and the whole thing fell apart, damn near got our asses busted too, man."

Father Bearald One did not inspire the demands of the tribal women, although he shares their enthusiasms, but he did concentrate on a crime which altered the outcome from potential violence to satire.

Father Bearald overheard a conversation at the center that several street skins were planning to enter the fur trade by force: to rob a furrier in an exclusive store downtown. Noon was the scheduled time, high noon, allowing one to two hours tribal time. The shaman waited in the store behind a rack of expensive fur coats. Three overweight street skins came through the door, stumbling over each other, and announced in hesitant voices, "this is ah ah ah st stick up. . . . st st stick em up."

White women, casual customers, smiled, blithe ornamental faces in the fur, and then continued browsing through the animals on the racks. A mink snapped back, a weasel hissed and disappeared in winter, beaver clapped from the water, rabbits screamed in the talons of an owl, and the fattest skin in the pride reached into his small snug front pocket for a revolver. The shaman focused on his hand; it swelled in his pocket. The skin tugged and tugged until the seam ripped and his swollen hand was free. The shaman focused on his fingers, which swelled too large to fit through the trigger housing on the revolver.

"This, this, this. . . ." stammered the skin while he shook his hand as if he had been struck by a poisonous snake. He could not speak without stammering, or finish a sentence, while the shaman dowser watched him from behind the racoons and silver fox.

Meanwhile, the other skins were attempting to load a station wagon with expensive fur coats, but most of what the two robbers trapped were coats returned in trade, and most of those furs were dropped on the floor and sidewalk in front of the store. With no more than six used coats plundered from the trade, the fur bandits drove in the stolen station wagon to a second stolen vehicle, a van, an elaborate plan, and then to their car. However, the shaman dowser inspired the skin bandits to fail. The three skins forgot where the stolen van was parked. Finding it on a side street, an hour later, they transferred the furs, but the ignition switch would not turn in the van. The key fit, but it would not turn.

"What are you doing in my van?" screamed a man coming out of a house near the van. "Get the hell out of my van. . . . Who are you?

"Shit, man."

"Forget the fur."

"Split, man."

The three bandit skins ran down the street, leaving the fur trade, station wagon, the van, and the keys behind. The crime had ended, some skins will tell, by chance, but the shaman dowser made these stories possible.

The bandit skins had pulled up behind the wrong van, same size, shape, and color, but the wrong van. The van, the furs, and the station wagon were returned. No one was hurt, and no skins were arrested. The white women never knew their furs were being plundered, never realized their exclusive roles in the new urban fur trade.

"That shaman gonna be our ruin, man."

"No way, man," said the board member in the black and blue ribbon shirt. "What's he done? So he wears an overshoe, what's that, man? He could be weird but where would we be without him now?"

"Listen, man, he goes."

"You better have good reasons to talk like that."

"Listen, man, that shaman messed with our election and you heard what he did with the door thing."

"What *door* thing?"

"He found out who did in the door, man."

"Man, *you* did. . . . big secret."

Father Bearald heard from the curator of the museum in the center that someone had a key to the video and sound booth where equipment had been stolen. The curator changed the locks but did not give the director a key. However, one morning the curator tried to open the door, but the only key to the booth did not work in the lock.

"He found out about *you*, man."

An investigation revealed that someone had chopped down the solid ten-foot cedar door to get at equipment in the booth and then replaced the felled door with a similar door from a different room in the center. The curator asked the shaman dowser if he could find the person who chopped down the door and stole a color television receiver, among other expensive items. The shaman dowser was known for his abilities to locate wild game and birds, and lost children. Having been lost himself, he knew where to look in his visions.

Father Bearald pictured in his mind the color television picture on the stolen receiver, and when he pictured a late night talk show, he used his beaver poplar dowsing stick to locate the house, like a wild animal, where the set was hidden. It turned out to be a member of the board, who later explained that he had borrowed the set to watch the national democratic convention in color at home.

"We gotta keep up in politics, man."

"But why chop down a door?" asked the man in the black and blue ribbon shirt. "Why fell a good cedar door for nothing?"

"Because it was there."

"What reason is that?"

"I chopped it down, man, to save it."

"Shit, *you* are weird."

"Man, that shaman is our ruin."

"You are our ruin."

"No, man, that shaman messed up our elections on the council. Television and doors, man, nothin compared to that shaman creep spookin people during our election speeches."

"Watch your tongue with a shaman."

"That's another thing."

"What?"

"My tongue."

"Yes, your tongue, it would be a public service if the shaman took it," said the man in the black and blue ribbon shirt. He had been pacing around the conference table in his usual manner, and then he stopped, a sudden stop, and looked out the window.

Father Bearald One was shuffling in his overshoe toward the entrance to the building. The Prospect Park American Indian Center had become his new dowser station, the sacred crossroad on his travels as a trickster, an appropriate place in the world of chance to outwit evil and balance the universe. But one universe he balanced, for the moment, caused the shaman dowser a minor imbalance in his own world, a "natural tilt" he said. Bearald was banished as a board member: voted in and out in less than two months, the shortest tenure on the board.

Father Bearald attended a series of speeches last week by radical incumbent skins who were running for reelection to the Urban Indian Tribal Council, an umbrella organization which received federal funds to plan and administer programs for urban tribal people, with or without their consent. The council was dominated by corrupt skins whom the trickster shaman inspired to be fools in public. The radical skins did not need much influence.

Father Bearald was blamed for causing a radical skin to curse the white man, when there were no white men present, and for causing skins to talk about tribal women as traditional servants of the new urban word warriors. The shaman dowser was blamed and burdened with the behavior of a mean urban tribal feminist, who leaped to the microphone and pulled the radical skin down to the floor with his two braids. Worlds reversed, the warrior was vulnerable in braids. In the wings, a third candidate and

EARTHDIVERS AT THE WORD CINEMAS

Spacious Treeline in Words

Between the too warm flesh of the literal event and the cold skin of the concept runs meaning. This is how it enters into the book. Everything enters into, transpires in the book. This is why the book is never finite. It always remains suffering and vigilant. . . . Every exit from the book is made within the book. . . . If writing is not a tearing of the self toward the other within a confession of infinite separation, if it is a delectation of itself, the pleasure of writing for its own sake, the satisfaction of the artist, then it destroys itself. . . . One emerges from the book, because . . . the book is not in the world, but the world is in the book.

Jacques Derrida, *Writing and Difference*

Holding forth at the spacious treelines with the bears and the crows, the best tellers in the tribes peel peel peel peel their words like oranges, down to the last navel. Mimicked in written forms over winter now, transposed in mythic metaphors, the interior glories from oral traditions burst in conversations and from old footprints on the trail.

"The text you write must prove to me *that it desires me,*" writes Roland Barthes in his book *The Pleasures of the Text.* "This proof exists: it is writing. Writing is: the science of the various blisses of language. . . . I am interested in language because it wounds or seduces me. . . . The language I speak *within myself* is not of my time; it is prey, by nature, to ideological suspicion; thus it is with this language that I must struggle. I write because I do not want the words I find. . . ."

The most imaginative tribal writers seldom peel peel peel peel their oranges at random, not even in the ritual darkness, but *untribal* translators and talebearers march march march their words down mission rows in perfect grammatical time, building word castles here and there in the sacred sand, territorial and colonial verbs, fabricating their words in prestressed phrases, interior mechanical landscapes, separating tribal orchards from the sacred. The written word leaves a different footprint near the treeline. The oral tradition is a visual event, but in written form stories are formed as scripts, struck into print from grammatical philosophies, so that the reader, trained to read with critical class expectations, becomes the master of sand castles, a teller and a listener in a single interior voice from a written template. The reader remembers footprints near the treeline, near the limits of understanding in written words, but the trail is never marked with printed words. The trail is made as a visual event between imaginative creators, tellers, and listeners: we hold our breath beneath the surface, the written word, but we know that respiration and transpiration are possible under water.

"The pleasure of the text is that moment when my body pursues its own ideas," writes Roland Barthes in *The Pleasure of the Text*, "for my body does not have the same ideas I do. . . . The pleasure of the text is not the pleasure of the corporeal striptease or of narrative suspense. In these cases, there is no tear, no edges: a gradual unveiling: the entire excitation takes refuge in the *hope* of seeing the sexual organ . . . or in knowing the end of the story. . . . Thus, what I enjoy in a narrative is not directly its content or even its structure, but rather the abrasions I impose upon the fine surface: I read on, I skip, I look up, I dip in again. Which has nothing to do with the deep laceration the text of bliss inflicts upon language itself, and not upon the simple temporality of its reading. . . ."

These imaginative narratives are written in double visions, peeled from visual experiences on the trail near the spacious treeline and transposed in tribal visual word cinemas. The four interior scenes, the stories within stories and between tellers and listeners, are satirical mind theaters staged at the crossroads near the orchards, near the windmills on distant moors, mountains, and in classrooms.

"The imagination is always aware of the present. . . ." writes Mary Warnock in her book *Imagination.* "Neither understanding alone nor sensation alone can do the work of imagination, nor can they be conceived to come together without imagination. . . . Only imagination is in this sense creative; only it makes pictures of things."

The scenes in these stories, in these word cinemas, are visual dream flights, untimed in unusual places, with terminal believers and urban shamans and landfill meditators. The word *indian* appears in lowercase letters in these stories.

CLASSROOM WINDMILLS

Tulip shares her dreams with me at dusk. She is fascinated with natural power, wind through windmills, the moon through pine boughs, white water down the mountain, salmon in the sun, crows over the prairie. She builds miniature windmills, and she has transformed our tribal resource center, one of several special ethnic libraries on campus, windows opened wide to the ocean, into a palace of whirrs and wind rattles.

Tulip reveals no secrets, and she bears no confessions from her tribal origins. She is more beautiful than the wind from all directions and she is my weakness, but her weakness has never been me. She has but one weakness, it is her pure hatred for indian men, parts of me included, mixedblood or whole; and, though she is obsessed with natural power, she is inhibited about the instinctive power of sex. Most offensive to her is the language of sex.

Tulip finds much more pleasure and awareness in water and wind than she does in masculine muscles or an erect penis. The copper blades on her miniature windmills, white water, sandpipers, wounded killdeer, the motions and sounds from the earth, morning in the cottonwoods, but not indian men, speak the natural languages she understands. Tulip trusts me, rather, she trusts the secrets and silence in me, and she shares her dreams with me when we are alone.

Histories harden like prairie mud and disappear in her memories. The first time we were together she was a flower, the wind was gentle over the meadow, and the shamans and the tribal clowns at the borders of sexual reversals burst over the earth, through the wet leaves in the summer ceremonies of the sun. Sexual contradictions are like the changes in the wind, enchanting, wind and rain on the leaves, the pleasures are tacit and preternatural. We touch with words, but she believes that the words on sex are demeaning, metaphors from violence and domination, reductions from natural experiences, the opposites from nurturance. She demands silence in sex, restraint like birds in magical flight, control, too much control, wordless and breathless at the most ecstatic moments. Not a thunderstorm in her, but a warm hesitant rain on the cedar and fern, no more than whispers. She is not a shadow, she is the moon.

Tulip has sound reasons to hate indian men. As a child, a beautiful natural creature like a fur salmon upstream, and as a young woman, she was abused by several indian men. Living in a small shack on the reservation, she watched drunken indian men lust for women, word pits, scored brown books, and she heard the harsh and violent sounds of sex over her mother and her sisters.

Tulip has the haunting face of a woodland animal, soft skin, smooth black hair. Her smile flickers from the first dream fires of the tribes. She chooses to be alone, to be silent, to live with secrets, to be with her winds like a windmill near the ocean. Tulip *is* the wind, she *is* nature, and I am a fool.

Tulip is in my dreams.

The sound of the windmills reminds me of her power.

Tulip is also a victim of what she remembers and avoids. Behind her desk, through a thin plaster wall in the next office, she can hear, three or four times a week, the uninhibited and unabashed sounds of wild sex.

SATIRICAL STALLION

Twice a week in the afternoon, two hours before his special seminar on tribal literature, Pink Stallion has loud sex with blondes in his office next to the tribal resource center. The windmills, even in a stiff wind, do not rise above the sounds of sex. Tulip cannot avoid hearing these smut events through the wall behind her desk.

"Blondes stimulate ideas," asserts the Pink Stallion.

When we hear blonde laughter coming through the thin wall from his office, moaning over the sound of the windmills, the center turns silent. Even the windmills seem to slow down to listen. Lips open and close with special care, books drop closed, pens poised, while we wait to hear the final cries from the blonde resurrection of General George Custer.

Tulip hears the first sounds near her desk. The opening of the couch against the wall, a thud, a moan, curses, hard breathing—all drive her to pack her books and wind charts and leave for her apartment in the hills. She dreams there, flashing her fur upstream in the sun.

Pink Stallion bridled his mixedblood horse in time for our seminar on tribal literature. Twice a week he appears with flush cheeks, lecture notes in hand. From the curve of his smile like a trickster he must know that we listen in on his time with blondes.

"This week," said Pink Stallion, opening the seminar, "we will discuss the meaning of culture, mythical opposition and resolution, sacred connections and secular separations, and experiences in the oral tradition, as discovered in several indian novels, and in *Landfill Meditation,* a collection of skin stories about an urban shaman."

"Shall we begin with these questions, please: What use is culture if it does not support our dreams and visions? As a form of consciousness, is culture a denial of mortality? The denial of the earth in us? Should we be at war, word wars in opposition with a culture that invalidates our dreams and visions?"

Silence.

We were bored; after the sounds of sex through the wall we were bored with seminars and trick questions. Bound in urban rituals, we were bored with words; material magic and street chatter limited our imagination. We were unable to respond to metaphors with more than passive political rhetoric and disconnected curses.

"Shit, man, culture? What culture you talkin on, brother?" carped Bad Mouth, the first and the last to speak. Her words were broken arrows. She resisted ideas, and from her passive resistance she found personal power in symbolic opposition. Mixedblood and urban, she was immortal in word wars.

Bad Mouth never reads. She frowns and sulks. She hates books, white people, and insects, in that order. The whirr and rattle of the miniature windmills sound to her like thousands of insects, and she hates the wind too because of the windmills. She prevails with hatred and insists that what sounds evil must be evil.

Pink Stallion resists the world in a different manner. When he was first asked to teach a seminar on indian literature for indians, he resisted because there would be no white students there, which meant in translation, no blondes. He called such a seminar "bone head literature for racists," but as the power of the indian students increased, he turned the indian seminar idea into an act of survival.

Pink Stallion leaned forward, mounted his white-framed reading glasses, and read from *Myth and Meaning* by Claude Lévi-Strauss: "Mythical stories are, or seem, arbitrary, meaningless, absurd, yet nevertheless they seem to reappear all over the world. . . . Each of us is a kind of crossroads where things happen. The crossroads is purely passive; something happens there. A different thing, equally valid, happens elsewhere. There is no choice, it is just a matter of chance."

Silence.

The students looked out the window.

The windmills whirred.

Pink Stallion looked out the window, looked toward the ocean with the students, while he continued his lecture: "The invented indian in us has become a perfect victim, separated from the living, an object with no sacrificial significance, *objet-trouvé,* a word icon, perfect inventions from romantic literature. The invented indian is thrown in us from a white wheel, a white ceramic creation without nurturance."

"You always talk about that shit, man, what white people are thinking, how about talking about what indians are thinking for a change?" demanded Injun Time, who was the brightest in a pride of tribal fools. She received an urban vision and was given her sacred pet name by the leader of the San Francisco Sun Dancers.

"Did you hear me?" asked Injun Time. "Why do you always quote white people? Quote some indians for a change."

"Language, as we have discussed it in the past, structures our perceptions of the world," Pink Stallion explained. Looking toward the ocean, he pinched his lips until the skin turned white.

"Did you hear me the second time?" demanded Injun Time. "How come you never find out anything that indians write and think about?"

"You are quite right, Miss Injun Time," said Pink Stallion, leaning back in his chair at the head of the seminar table. His eyes returned from the ocean. "Your timing is perfect, because, it is now the time and place to consider indian authors, but first, let me make a check around the room to see who has read the indian materials."

Silence.

Fast Food, short, fat, and flush, true to his urban dream name, was the first to respond while he munched on corn chips. He brushed the crumbs from the seminar table in front of him, and mumbled that he had not read "all of the stuff, the stories."

"Which parts did you read?"

"The best parts that are indian."

"Name one part."

"Sure, the part where the white man gets what he's got coming to him, that's the part that I liked the best," said Fast Food.

Token White, lips and cheeks twitching from the opposition in her consciousness between tribal traditions and her word place in the urban world, said that she had read the stories, but she wished that she had not done so, because, she explained, indian author or not, she thought the tribal people in the stories were made to look foolish.

"Have you ever heard of satire?"

"Satire is not sacred," answered Token White, fulfilling the meaning of her romantic name. The students used their descriptive pet names from the urban sun dance. Token White stands tall, white, angular, absorbed in indian dreams, and tribal by serious practice.

"Mother earth is satire," said Pink Stallion.

"No, never," said Token White.

"Never, never," said Fine Print, moving his lips in silent recitation, passive and distant. He confessed that he was not a reader, never read prose, he explained, because prose is not traditional and because he is a writer of poems. The manner in which some students avoid linear thinking is linear.

Bad Mouth, slouching in her chair, sneered behind dark sunglasses, curled her upper lip, and cursed. "Shit, man, it never mean nothin to me, no how, man, indians never write that shit, man, indians got an oral tradition, man." Bad Mouth survived in the world with hatred. Invectives were the source of her urban visions, and her dream name, but she has not been an indian for long, which makes it difficult to know where and when the indian hatred begins and ends. Three years ago when her mother told her that her grandmother was a mixedblood indian from Mission La Soledad, Bad Mouth demanded that the Bureau of Indian Affairs make her an indian and give her a scholarship to college. Before her indian enlightenment she told her friends that her parents were both Maoris from New Zealand. "The third world is all the same," she said, and boasted that her father was a leader in the Northern California Hau Hau Movement, a sort of sacred urban cargo cult.

"What was that?"

"Shit, man, third world, man."

"Third world where?" asked Pink Stallion.

"Right here, man, shit." Bad Mouth was scheduled to graduate at the end of this quarter, but Rubie Blue Welcome failed her ass in a seminar on tribal languages, which is a degree requirement in indian studies. She did not wait long on the rim. With Doc Cloud Burst and the San Francisco Sun Dancers, Bad Mouth is leading a movement to control the department with urban indian spiritual power and eliminate the courses she did not pass.

Touch Tone, in braids and plastic bear claws, could have been named for plastic, but because he is best known for his long distance telephone conversations back to the reservation, he was named in a dream for the fastest dial. Wherever he visits he leaves a trail of long distance telephone bills. Aiming his water pistol around the room, he said he never did read what the indians wrote because indians live in oral traditions, and a real indian teacher would tell stories and not make indians read stories, "what is there to read in the indian world?"

"Perceptive question," said Pink Stallion.

"Shapersons are the best writers," said Injun Time. She tells stories with the voice of a shaman, or as she insists, a "shaperson." She sees auras and speaks about magical flights to other worlds where she learned the languages of plants and animals and birds. She knows about animals, and medicines from plants. Animals come to her on the streets and tell her stories, complain about their health in the cities, and laugh about their foolishness. Injun Time bears vitamins in her medicine bundle, a common practice among the members of the San Francisco Sun Dancers.

"When indians write, indians write," said Injun Time, fingering her leather medicine bundle around her neck, "and when indians read, indians read, and when this indian reads she reads what she likes to read, and she likes the short stories she read about the landfill meditator because he had a shit load of visions."

Silence.

The windmills whirred.

Injun Time smiled.

Pink Stallion slapped his thighs.

Transformations are not uncommon in the tribal world. Pink Stallion wished that he could become a large bird or a dark bear during his special seminar for indian students and flash his fur on the wind. He appeared now, chin in hand, to be soaring, but he explained later that he was transfixed with boredom and repressed hostilities about some of the indian students. "Tulip is a shorebird, and she transforms me from boredom with her windmills," he said, but then he changed her metaphor to a small animal, one he could mount no doubt.

"Have teachers become the ceremonial victims," Pink Stallion whispered over the windmills, and then he bounced from his hands and pawed through his notes and papers like a bear at a picnic.

"In time, all in good time, now, let me show all of you fine oral scholars, avid readers of indian literature, how to read, since this is your seminar and my survival," said Pink Stallion, turning the page in a collection of short stories written by indians.

"*Landfill Meditation* has an outside and an interior observer, or an omniscient narrator who goes for it and knows what is coming down. The story starts with a teacher telling stories and then one voice leads to another, as stories did in the oral tradition, from teller to listener to listener and more. We move through time with a shaman until the end when the writer delivers us back to the classroom where we started as readers and listeners. These stories take place in a house of word mirrors, with the denouement being little more than the return of the narrator to our interior space."

"Shit, man. . . ."

"Shit, what, woman," responded Pink Stallion.

"Shit, man, you done teaching here."

"We were *done* when we were invented," countermoved the Pink Stallion from behind the windmills. He remounted his reading glasses and cleared his throat. "These *Landfill Meditation* stories begin with Clement Beaulieu, a mixedblood character from the White Earth Reservation in Minnesota. Beaulieu conducts seminars on Native American philosophies and tribal meditation, environmental fantasies, animal languages, and talking and walking backward, one night each week at Shaman High, which, as you know, is a transcendental college in Marin County, California.

Bad Mouth stopped two windmills before she shouldered her red pack, and leaving the seminar and cultural resource center, she slammed the door three times.

Injun Time straightened the blades on the windmills.

Pink Stallion looked out toward the setting sun over the ocean. The wind was cool on his face, and he remembered the stories he would tell about the urban shaman teacher. He looked down at his book and began to read about landfill meditation and tribal transformations.

The windmills whirred in time.

Bad Mouth returned to the seminar table, mean as ever, with three new urban sun dancers to hold her evil line.

URBAN SHAMANS

Last week, when the teaching trickster entered the classroom, conversations stopped in the middle of sentences. He removed his leather coat with unusual caution, walked backward moving his head from side to side like an animal at the shoreline, smiled, turned out the overhead fluorescent lights, and then he waited near the open window in silence. There, in his woodland visions, he followed the water moons backward over the mountains on familiar tribal vision faces. Traffic over the Golden Gate Bridge roared down the word maps and sacred place names in the distance.

Pink Stallion stopped reading and looked around the table to see who was listening. Fast Food was munching corn chips as usual. Touch Tone was sleeping with his head back and his mouth wide open.

"How does he know that sacred stuff?" asked Token White, strumming the sinew on her favorite bow.

"Sacred memories."

"But his stories are like entertainment," Token White insisted. "How can that stuff be sacred?"

"Memories have no unconscious forms," explained Pink Stallion. "Entertainment is not a categorical experience because we seldom remember events in forms."

"What was that?"

"When we tell about our experiences we remember events outside the forms in which the experiences first occurred."

"Shit, man."

"Remember sex first and the backseat later."

"Now we meet the characters in the stories," said Pink Stallion. The trickster told stories backward about the four directions and the four tribal characters who traveled with him that night from the window: Martin Bear Charme the landfill meditator, Happie Comes Last the demure gossiper, Oh Shinnah Fast Wolf the metatribal moralist, and Belladonna Winter Catcher the roadwoman with terminal creeds.

The following is an imaginative translation from the *drawkcab,* or backward patois, in which these stories were first told and recorded:

"Backward what?" asked Token White.

"*Patois* means a special language, street talk, for example, or a common dialect which is different from the standard language," explained Pink Stallion.

Martin Bear Charme owns a reservation, the teaching trickster told backward from the darkness, teaches a seminar on refuse meditation, and circumscribes his own unusual images in the material world.

Charme commands us to believe that imaginative meditation means walking backward through the refuse and telling visual stories to writers who never take notes, but not, he said twice, but not speaking to be recorded or smiling to be photographed.

Words are rituals in the oral tradition, from the knowledge of creation, little visions on the winds, said the old tribal scavenger to his students, not electronic sounds separating the tellers from the listeners. Landfill meditation restores the connections between refuse and the refuser.

Charme, mixedblood master meditator who tells that he walked backward down from Turtle Mountain Reservation in North Dakota, is much more vain than astute about his photogenic face and emulsion visage. He has an enormous nose attached to his smooth face, and in his stare is the power of the bear.

Oh Shinnah Fast Wolf, autonomous mistress of metatribal ceremonies, started soughing on stage at the Unitarian Church in Berkeley under the sounds of automobile traffic, about the guardians at the heart of mother earth, while a disciple in sparrow feathers, bearing a pacific smile, held open the double doors for one more cash contribution to balance the earth at the fault.

"Shit, man," said Bad Mouth.

"She did not explain her identities," said Pink Stallion who was at the meeting, filled with cedar smoke and terminal believers, "but she said she was authorized to speak for mother earth."

Happie Comes Last, reservation born laborer in a healthfood cooperative, a horsewoman, and columnist for the *Mountain Meditator*, a critical tabloid on meditation and holistic healing, would have been the last cash donor, but there at the double doors, sorting through the cards and letters in her leather pouch like a marsupial, she found a free press ticket and a caricature of the refuse meditation leader. Flashing the ticket and caricature, she asked the disciple, as she moved beneath his feathers and outstretched arms, where was the refuse meditator sitting?

Charme sits over there, the disciple said, pointing with his chin and blond head; he is in the white pants, the one with the oil on his nose, in the back near the window.

Comes Last leaned back to gossip with the attractive blond disciple: Did you know that he walks and talks backward? He never answers interviews but in public places like this.

No, the blond disciple whispered back over his shoulder, where are his private places?

Martin Bear Charme, founder of the Landfill Meditation Reservation and the seminar with the same name, scooped the oil from his outsized nose with his dark middle finger, his habit once or twice an hour, and spread the viscid mounds over his cuticles. Sitting near the window, one would never know, watching his smooth hands in backward speech, that the refuse meditator was reservation born, once poor, and undereducated for urban survival.

"Right on, man," exclaimed Fast Food.

Nose Charmer, his tribal pet name on the reservation, hitchhiked to San Francisco when he was sixteen and settled in a waterfront hotel. He studied welding on a federal relocation program, but scrap connections bored him so he turned to scavenging and made a fortune hauling and filling wetlands with solid waste and urban swill. Once a worthless mud flat, his lush refuse reservation on South San Francisco Bay near Mountain View is now worth millions.

Charme and his legal advisor, Bicker Becker, have petitioned the federal government for recognition of the reservation as a sovereign tax-free tribal meditation nation, a place where laws and liens are intuitive. Petulant Becker, titular dean of the California Meditation and Levitation Law School, argues that even individuals in shamanic flight and astral projections should be recognized as duty-free ports.

There never was refuse like this on the reservation, Charme told his seminar, because on the old reservations *we* were the refuse, *we* were the waste, solid and swill on the run, telling stories from a discarded culture to amuse the colonial refusers.

The blond disciple dropped his arms and his smile, and the double doors wagged closed on the traffic sounds. Oh Shinnah, her hair bound back in tight braids, cut counter shapes around her head in abstruse hand rituals and then snapped two match heads together four times, igniting a small cedar bundle in front of her on the floor.

Comes Last, smiling and nodding with embarrassment, broke through the silent aisles while the little chapel filled with thick sweet smoke. Down the back row she cleared her throat and then perched on the last chair, not knowing that the old scavenger commanded the last place near the window, his escape distance from spiritual faults.

Chanting *wanaki nimiwin wanaki*, Charme scooped his nose oil once more while Oh Shinnah focused on the visions in her crystal ball, and then in perfect tribal trickster time he rolled with his chair past Comes Last in magical flight toward the window, a movement she later described in her column as *soaring backward on a shaman chair.*

Pink Stallion paused to tell us that he was there too, at the meeting, sitting near the shaman in the back of the chapel. He explained that magical flight was a common shamanic tribal experience, moving through other times and places, other lives and spaces in creation.

"Shaman understand the language, what was that word about special languages?" asked Injun Time.

"Patois."

"Shaman understand animal and plant patois too, but what do the indian words mean, the ones you told?"

"*Wanaki* means peace and *nimiwin* means dancing, in the tribal language of the *anishinaabe,*" said Pink Stallion. He continued reading.

The first time Comes Last called on the refuse meditator at his urban reservation he was sitting in a room filled with trash. She asked him about his place of birth and his theories on the mind, but he said nothing more than *wanaki nimiwin wanaki*. She asked questions four times before leaving his reservation.

Martin Bear Charme smiled, nodded his head four times backward, and then laughed, throwing his nose back like a bear at the tree line ha ha ha haaaa.

Looking up from her ball and turtle fetish, Oh Shinnah stopped her invocation on mother earth between the words *intuition* and *compassion* to explain that she had serious business on her mind and in her heart about mineral companies and progressive reservation governments, and, she said, *we* will *not* compete with the animals.

Pink Stallion added that several animals were walking around the chapel, panting, snorting, and thumping on the wooden floor, which interrupted the speaker.

"I was sitting near the window, in the back where Martin Bear Charme soared backward," said Pink Stallion. "A calico cat leaped through the opened window into my lap. Well, I was startled, but being around so many shamans, I pretended that cats come to me all the time." The truth is that Pink Stallion hates cats, but cats seem attracted to him.

Wanaki nimiwin wanaki ha ha ha haaaa, Charme chanted, throwing his voice backward from his escape distance near the window.

Who would believe you were a meditator, tribal no less, Comes Last whispered out of the side of her mouth. She shifted from side to side on her perch. She is a bird who appears perched wherever and on whatever she sits. When she speaks she thrusts her lips out like a beak, giving rise to her sickle feathers, an avian illusion in the willows.

What does it mean?

What does *it* mean?

Wanaki nimiwin wanaki over and over.

Four skins lost in dreams ha ha ha haaaa.

Not foreskins, she said through her tense lips, indians never did circumcisions, tell the truth now, what does it mean?

"Shit, man, real indians never talk like that, man," snapped Bad Mouth as she shouldered her red pack. She slammed her chair to the table, stopped several windmills again, slammed her chair to the table, and then slammed the door when she left the resource center with her three urban sun dance followers.

Wanaki peaceful place, *nimiwin wanaki* dancing in a peaceful place ha ha ha haaaa, said the landfill meditator to the bird sitting near the window.

Where?

Landfill and summer swill.

Talk sense, Comes Last demanded, opening her leather-bound notebook. How are those words spelled? she asked.

D R A W K C A B N A M A H S

Mister Charme, she said, shifting her head to the side to see his nose, what does it mean, landfill meditation? Please in a phrase or two, speak slow now.

Unstable.

Unstable what?

Unstable in an earthquake.

Be serious, please.

Stable.

Stable what?

Stable on a windmill in a mindswell.

Never mind, she said, closing her leather notebook. Damn fool, what do you know about meditation? Nothing!

Refuse meditation cures cancer with visions. Some people clean their kitchens better than others too, said the solid waste magnate.

Mister Charme, please, you are speaking to a healthfood worker, she said, brushing lumps of leather from her black dress, not one of your meditation victims.

Charme scooped the oil from his nose and continued. Clean minds and clean kitchens are delusions, unrewarded altruism. When our visions are clean we seem to feel much better, but no less insecure.

Comes Last turned her head, avoiding the meditator, pretending not to be interested in what he was telling. Stop talking at me, she said, bouncing in her chair.

But you listen so much better when you are not listening to me ha ha ha haaaa. Pretend you are not interested.

Damn fool.

Once upon a time taking out the garbage was an event in our lives, a state of being connected to action. We were part of the rituals connecting us to the earth, from the places food grew through the house and our bodies, and then back to the earth. Garbage was real, part of creation, not an objective invasion of cans and cartons.

Refuse meditation teaches us to turn the mind back to the earth through the visions of real waste, the trash meditator continued.

His voice distracted the celebrants sitting in the next row. Faces turned and scowled. The old scavenger smiled back and resumed his stories.

We are the garbage, the waste, we make it and dump it, to be separated from it is a cancer-causing delusion, he said, but with some doubt in the tone of his voice. We cannot separate ourselves clean and perfect by dumping our trash out back. The earth is a victim of our internal trash.

Pink Stallion pointed out certain ironies and the references to ideas derived from meditation and holistic health. "The earth has become a sacrificial victim," he said, "because the white man has lost his mythic connections with the earth, like families abandoned on the interstates."

Stop this now, Comes Last insisted. You made your fortune on trash, and now you are making me sick with it. Let me sit here now and not listen to you.

Sickness is one of the best meditation experiences. Think about being sick, focus on your stuffed nose, make your mind an unclean kitchen. Now, said the old scavenger, rather than hating to clean up the kitchen, making it smell different, get right down with the odors. Focus on the odors in the corners, take the odors in, you know, the same way we smell our underarms and feet, because *we* are the bad smells we smell separated from our own real kitchens in the mind.

What was that?

Never mind . . . and the clean words that part us from the real smells leave us defensive victims of fetid swill and cancer. Take on odors in the same way we take on what we fear, become the opposition, become the swill. Did you understand that part? Ha ha ha haaaa.

You are sick, what you need are some clean words in your head, said Comes Last, moving two chairs down the back row out of his bad breath range.

Cancer is first a word, nothing more, a separation without vision, he said, following her down the row. We are culture bound to be clean, but being clean is a delusion and a separation from the visual energies of the earth. Holistic health is a harmonious vision, not an aromatic word prison.

Listen, we are the dreamers for the earth, he said in a deep voice. Turning down the dreams with clean words, defensive terminal creeds, earth separations, denies odors and death and causes cancer.

The celebrants turned toward the old scavenger in the back row and told him to be silent. One woman wagged her hand at him, warning him not to speak about diseases during sacred ceremonies in the cedar smoke.

We are death, said the refuse meditator to the woman in the next row. Unabashed, he stood and spoke in a loud voice to all the celebrants in the chapel. We are rituals, not perfect words; we are the ceremonies, not the witnesses, that connect us to the earth. We are the earth dreamers, the holistic waste, not the detached nose pinchers between the refuse and the refusers.

Go to a place in the waste to meditate, chanted the refuse meditator. Come to our reservation on the landfill to focus on waste and transcend the ideal word worlds, clean talk and terminal creeds, and the disunion between the mind and the earth. Come meditate on trash and swill odors and become the waste that holds us to the earth.

Injun Time asked Pink Stallion to read that paragraph again. "The one about clean talk and terminal creeds. . . . That man must be a word skin."

Go to a place in the waste to meditate. . . . Focus on waste and transcend the ideal word worlds, clean talk and terminal creeds, and the disunion between the mind and the earth. . . .

Pipe down in the back.

Oh Shinnah raised an eagle feather and told the mother earth celebrants that her feather made her tell the truth; should I not speak straight, the feather will tremble. Now listen, we live in a retarded country. . . . we vote for a peanut picker looking for a way to freedom and look where we have come. People are tearing up our land without examining it.

Hang with mother earth, she said, raising her fist; if the four corners tribal land is destroyed, then purification comes with a closed fist. If the electromagnetic pole at the four corners is upset, the earth will slip in space, causing the death of two-thirds of the population, no matter where you go to hide.

Oh Shinnah makes more sense with cedar smoke and fetishes than you do with all that double back talk about meditation, Comes Last declared, raising her chin.

Silence.

The lights flickered several times, and then out. The celebrants whispered in the darkness until the smell of cedar smoke in the chapel turned to the odor of landfill swill, or what Comes Last described in her column as a mixture of human excrement and dead animals. At first whiff the celebrants took cover in clean words, thinking the person next in row had passed bad air. But later, when the chapel filled with the scent of wild flowers, one celebrant allowed how terrible was the smell. While the others praised the passing of the bad odors, Comes Last, whose nose had not separated from the world of animals, smelled a bear in the darkness.

Listen ha ha ha haaaa.

Martin Bear Charme moved around the chapel in the darkness, from row to row and chair to chair, telling stories about terminal creeds. His voice seemed to rise and waver from the four directions. Words dropped from the beams, sounds came from under the chairs, and several celebrants were certain that the stories he told that night were told inside their own heads.

Listen ha ha ha haaaa.

Pink Stallion paused once more to explain how the author shifted to a different time and place. "We started out at a seminar, then moved to a church, and then to the landfill reservation, back to the church, and now to a place, as you will hear in a moment, named Orion, which is a town framed in red bricks and a constellation showing the figure of a hunter with a sword."

TERMINAL CREEDS

Orion was framed in a great wall of red earthen bricks, said the refuse meditator. Within the red walls lived several families who were descendants of famous hunters and western bucking horse breeders. Like good horses, the sign outside the walls said, proud people keep to themselves and their own breed, but from time to time we invite others to share food and conversation.

Belladonna Winter Catcher, who was born and conceived at Wounded Knee, her traveling companion Catholic Bishop Omax Parasimo, and several other tribal pilgrims knocked at the gate. We are tribal mixedbloods with good stories and memories from thousands of good listeners. Open the gate and let us in or we will blow your house down.

Listen to this, said Belladonna who was reading the sign on the red wall: *Terminal Creeds are Terminal Diseases. . . . The Mind is the Perfect Hunter and Narcissism is a Form of Isolation.*

The metal portcullis opened, and several guards dressed in uniforms escorted the pilgrims through the red wall. The pilgrims were examined. Information was recorded about birth places, education and experiences, travels and diseases, attitudes on women and politics. The hunters and breeders welcomed the visitors to tell stories about what was happening in the world outside the walls.

The pilgrims followed the hunters and breeders through the small town to one of the large houses where dozens of people were waiting on the front steps. Introductions and questions about political views were repeated again and again.

Thousands of questions were asked before dinner was served in the church dining room. Bishop Parasimo was the first to shift the flow of conversations. He asked the hunters and breeders sitting at his table to discuss the meaning of the messages on the outside walls. What does it mean, narcissism is a form of isolation? Please explain how the mind is the perfect hunter.

Narcissism rules the possessor, said a breeder with a deep scar on the side of his forehead. Narcissism is the fine art that turns the dreamer into paste and ashes.

The perfect hunter leaves himself and becomes the animal or bird he is hunting, said a hunter on the other side of the table. He touched his ear with his curled trigger finger as he spoke. The perfect hunter turns on himself, hunts himself in his mind. He lives on the edge of his own meaning, the edge of his own humor. He is the hunter and the hunted at the same time.

The breeders and hunters at the table smiled and nodded and then turned toward the head table where the bald banker breeder was tapping his water glass. Belladonna was sitting next to the banker. Her nervous fingers fumbled with the two beaded necklaces around her neck.

The families applauded when the banker spoke of their mission against terminal creeds. Depersonalize the word in the world of terminal believers, and we can all share the good side of humor. . . . Terminal believers must be changed or driven from our dreams.

Belladonna could feel the moisture from his hand resting on her shoulder. He referred to her as the good spirited speaker who has traveled through the world of savage lust on the interstates, this serious tribal woman, our speaker from the outside world, who once carried with her a tame white bird.

Belladonna leaned back in her chair. Her thighs twitched from his words about the tame white bird. The banker did not explain how he knew that she once lived with a dove. The medicine man told her it was an evil white witch so she turned the dove loose in the woods, but the bird returned. She cursed the bird and locked it out of her house, but the white dove soared in crude domestic circles and hit the windows. The dove would not leave. One night, when she was alone, she squeezed the bird in both hands, but the dove seemed content. She shook the dove. Behind the house, against a red pine, she severed the head of the white dove with an ax. Blood spurted in her face. The headless dove flopped backward into the dark woods.

We are waiting, said the banker.

Belladonna shivered near her chair, chasing the dove from her memories. She fumbled with her neck beads. Tribal values and dreams is what I will talk about.

Speak up . . . speak up.

Tribal values is the subject of my talk, she said in a louder voice. She dropped her hands from her beads. We are raised with values that shape our world in a different light. . . . We are tribal and that means that we are children of dreams and visions. Our bodies are connected to mother earth, and our minds are the clouds. Our voices are the living breath of the wilderness.

My grandfathers were hunters, said the hunter with the trigger finger at his ear. They said the same thing about the hunt that you said is tribal, so what does that mean?

I am different from a whiteman because of my values, she said. I would not be white, never white.

Do tell me, said an old woman breeder in the back of the room. We can see that you are different from a man, but tell us please how you are so different from *white people*.

We are different because we are raised with different values, Belladonna explained. She was fumbling with her beads again. Our parents treat us different as children. We are not punished. We live in larger families and never send our old people to homes to be alone. These are some things that make us different.

More, more.

Tribal people seldom touch each other, said Belladonna. She folded her hands over her breasts. We do not invade the personal bodies of others, and we do not stare at people when we are talking. . . . Indians have more magic in their lives.

Wait a minute, hold on there, said a hunter with an orange beard. Let me find something out here before you make me so different from the rest of the world. Tell me about this word *indian* that you use, tell me which *indians* are you talking about, or for, or are you talking for all *indians*? And if you are speaking for all *indians*, then how can there be truth in what you say?

Indians have their religion in common.

What does *indian* mean?

Are you so stupid that you cannot figure out what and who indians are? An indian is a member of a tribe and a person who has indian blood.

But what is *indian* blood?

Indian blood is not white blood.

Inventions, that must be what *indians* are, inventions, said the hunter with the beard. You tell me that the invention is different from the rest of the world when it was the rest of the world that invented the *indian*, right here on this land. We invented you and that must be why you hate us so much, because you have taken to believe in the invention. An *indian* is an *indian* because he speaks and thinks and believes he is an *indian* . . . The invention must not be so bad because the tribes have taken it up for keeps.

Mister, does it make much difference what the word *indian* means when I tell you from my heart that I have always been proud that I am an indian, said Belladonna. Proud to speak the voice of mother earth.

Please continue.

Well, as I was explaining, tribal people are closer to the earth, to the meaning and energies of the woodlands and the mountains and the plains. . . . We are not a competitive people like the whites who competed this nation into corruption and failure.

When you use the plural pronoun, asked a woman hunter with short white hair, does that mean that you are talking for all tribal people?

Fine Print leaned forward at the seminar table, moved his lips in silence for a minute or two and then asked: "What is all that shit about grammar, anyway?"

Most of them.

How about the western fishing tribes, the old tribes, the tribes that burned down their own houses in potlatch ceremonies?

Exceptions are not the rule.

Fools never make rules, said the woman with white hair. You speak from terminal creeds, not as a person of real experiences and critical substance.

Thank you for the meal, said Belladonna. She smirked and turned in disgust from the hunters and breeders. The banker placed his moist hand on her shoulder. Now, now, she will speak in good faith, said the banker, if you will listen with less critical ears. She does not want to debate her ideas. Give her another good hand. The hunters and breeders applauded. She smiled, accepted apologies, and started again.

The tribal past, our religion and dreams and the concept of mother earth, is precious to me. Living is not important if it is turned into competition and material gain. . . . Living is hearing the wind and speaking the languages of animals and soaring with eagles in magical flight. When I speak about these experiences it makes me feel powerful: the power of tribal religion and spiritual beliefs gives me protection. My tribal blood is like the great red wall you have around you here. . . . My blood moves in the circles of mother earth and through dreams without time. My tribal blood is timeless, and it gives me strength to live and deal with evil.

Right on sister, right on, said the hunter with the trigger finger on his ear. He leaped to his feet and cheered for her views.

"Right on, sister," chimed Token White.

"Four skins win," said Touch Tone, nodding his loose head in agreement as he shot spurts of sacred water in the air with his red water pistol.

Pink Stallion continued reading.

Powerful speech, said a breeder.

She deserves her favorite dessert, said a hunter in a deep voice. The hunters and breeders do not trust those narcissistic persons who accept personal praise.

Shall we offer our special dessert to this innocent child? asked the breeder banker. Let me hear it now, those who think she deserves her dessert, thank you, and now those who think she does not deserve dessert for her excellent speech.

No dessert please, said Belladonna.

Fast Food said, "give it to me, then."

Now, now, how could you turn down the enthusiasm of the hunters and breeders who listened to your thoughts here? How could you turn down their vote for your dessert?

The hunters and breeders cheered and whistled when the cookies were served. The circus pilgrims were not comfortable with the shift in moods, the excessive enthusiasm.

The energies here are strange, said Bishop Omax Parasimo up his sleeve. What does all this cheering mean?

Quite simple, said the breeder with the scar. You see, when questions are unanswered and there is no humor, the messages become terminal creeds, and the good hunters and breeders here seek nothing that is terminal. Terminal creeds are terminal diseases, and we celebrate when death is inevitable.

The families smiled when she stood to tell them how much she loved their enthusiasm. In your smiling faces I can see myself, she said. This is a good place to be, you care for the living. The hunters and breeders cheered again.

But you applaud her narcissism, said the bishop to the breeder with the scar. His hands were folded in a neat pile on the table.

She has demanded that we see her narcissism, said the breeder.

You heard her tell us that she did not like questions, different views; she is her own victim, a terminal believer.

But we are all victims.

The histories of tribal cultures have been terminal creeds and narcissistic revisionism, said the breeder. The tribes were perfect victims: if they had more humor and less false pride, the families would not have collapsed under so little pressure from the white man. . . . Show me a solid culture that disintegrates under the plow and the rifle and the saw.

Token White pounded on the table.

Pink Stallion stopped for a few minutes, looked around the table at the students, and then continued reading in a much louder voice to the end of the stories.

Your views are terminal.

Who is serious about the perfections of the past? Who gathers around them the frail hopes and febrile dreams and tarnished mother earth words? asked the hunter with the scar. Surviving in the present means giving up on the burdens of the past and the cultures of tribal narcissism.

Belladonna nibbled at her sugar cookie like a proud rodent. Her cheeks were filled and flushed. Her tongue tingled from the tartness of the cookie. In the kitchen the cooks had covered her cookie with a granulated time release alkaloid poison that would soon dissolve. The poison cookie was the special dessert for narcissists and believers in terminal creeds. She was her own perfect victim. The hunters and breeders have poisoned dozens of terminal believers in the past few months. Most of them were tribal people.

Fine Print cursed white people.

Token White strummed the sinew on her bow.

Belladonna nibbled at the poison dessert cookie, her polite response to the enthusiasm of the people who lived behind the wall. She smiled and nodded to the hunters and breeders who all watched her eat the last crumb.

The sun dropped beneath the great red earthen wall when the pilgrims passed through the gate. The pilgrims were silent, walking through the shadows. Seven crows circled until it was dark.

Belladonna was chanting her words. My father took me into the sacred hills. We started when the sun was setting because Old Winter Catcher had to know what the setting sun looked like before he climbed into the hills for the night. The sun was beautiful; it spread great beams of orange and rose colors across the heavens. My father said it was a good sunset. No haze to hide the stars. He said it was good, and we climbed into the hills. It feels like that time now; we are climbing into the hills for the visions of the morning.

We walked up part of the hill backward, Belladonna said with her head turned backward. Then he told me that the world is not as it appears to be frontward, not then, not now. To leave the world and to see the power of the spirit on the hills we had to walk out of the known world backward. We had to walk backward so nothing would follow us up the hill.

My father said that things that follow are things that demand attention. Do you think we are being followed now?

No, said Bishop Omax Parasimo, looking behind.

When I do this we are walking and talking into the morning with Old Winter Catcher, she said, walking and talking backward down the road: *noitnetta ruo no sdnamed on htiw gninrom otni emoc ot tsrif eht*

Fast Food asked for a translation.

the first to come into morning with no demands on our attention

Shaman High smelled of wild flowers and bears and landfill swill when the teaching trickster stopped his stories, and then soared backward out the window in the darkness and laughed ha ha ha haaaa over the mountains and familiar tribal faces on the woodland water moons.

Pink Stallion removed his reading glasses, bundled his books and papers under his arm, laughed ha ha ha haaaa, and then walked backward from the seminar table in the resource center through tribal fantasies and backward through the whirr and rattle of windmills, backward from the present to his appointment with a blonde in his office next door.

The windmills whirred.

Backward through the door he slammed the door.

The windmills whirred.

The students and mythic memories from the stories hunkered out of time near the thin wall and waited to hear the familiar pleasure moans and sex sounds of the Pink Stallion mounting the resurrection of General George Armstrong Custer in the office next door. The Little Bighorn loomed in primal dreams of tribal vengeance.

The windmills whirred while the students shared new trickeries and terminal resurrections and turned from their remembered past to mount the blondes on campus for the last ride home.